SIMON
SAYS

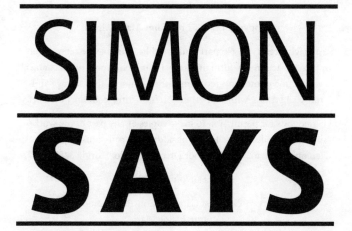

SIMON
SAYS

Elaine Marie Alphin

HARCOURT, INC.

San Diego   New York   London

Requests for permission to make copies of any part of the work
should be mailed to the following address: Permissions Department,
Harcourt, Inc., 6277 Sea Harbor Drive, Orlando, Florida 32887-6777.

www.HarcourtBooks.com

Library of Congress Cataloging-in-Publication Data
Alphin, Elaine Marie.
Simon says/by Elaine Marie Alphin.
p.   cm.
Summary: An alienated, aspiring young painter who attends
high school at a boarding school for the arts discovers that being
true to himself means opening the door to both pain and pleasure.
[1. Boarding schools—Fiction.   2. Identity—Fiction.   3. Painting—
Fiction.   4. Artists—Fiction.   5. Schools—Fiction.]   I. Title.
PZ7.A4625Si   2002
[Fic]—dc21   2001004967
ISBN 0-15-216355-7

Text set in Minion
Display set in Quay Sans
Designed by Cathy Riggs

First edition
C E G H F D B
Printed in the United States of America

*This is a work of fiction. All the names, characters, and events portrayed
in this book are the product of the author's imagination. Any resemblance
to any event or actual person, living or dead, is unintended.*

For Karla, who was there at the start.

For Charles, who was there at the end.

And for Art, who will always be there for me.

SIMON
SAYS

═══

A white petal ruffled in the breeze, then tore free from the wilting carnation on the student's grave and tumbled away. At first flowers appeared daily, loose handfuls, and even real bouquets. Then summer began, and visitors came to the church cemetery near the school campus less often. By the fall semester, old students had forgotten him, and new students wondered who he'd been. They had their own art to create, after all. He might have been special—but he was dead.

One student still came, however, not often, but occasionally. He sat on the grass and looked at the mounded earth, and sometimes spoke softly. One mild dawn, he dug into the sod beside the plain gravestone and buried, as far down as he could reach, a circular metallic disc wrapped in a few folded sheets of paper. Later, rain filled the loosely packed hole with mud and silt, and erased the faint hollow.

The dead student's name became a school story, part legend and part warning. The boy he had been, however, and the man he might have grown to be, were both forgotten. . . . Except by his murderer.

PART ONE

FALL

1

The mirror acts like a frame. But I would never paint on a shiny, reflective surface like that. Canvas draws the paint into it, draws the eye into it, draws the mind into its world. Mirrored glass shows too much, and too little. I came here to get away from games played with mirrors.

I always knew there had to be someone else who saw the games for what they were, someone else who hated them as much as I do. That's why I came to Whitman High School for the Arts—to meet this person. Only now I'm not so sure. Why should he care about meeting me?

"Well, Charles, are you coming or not?" Adrian demands. His voice fills our dorm room, easy and amused, blue-green tones flecked with golden highlights. "This was your idea, remember."

I remember. In the mirror I see sweaty fingers wiping themselves on a T-shirt as if they were paint-smeared, then fumbling to smooth the stretched-out cotton. Above the fingers I see frowning eyes that might be mistaken for angry instead of nervous.

"Having second thoughts?" asks Adrian.

I grab a rust-colored flannel shirt and shrug into it, letting it hang open over the T-shirt. Glancing in the mirror one last time, I meet my new roommate's hazel eyes. Sleek in black jeans and an open-necked gray shirt, a plaid so fine it looks like graph paper, Adrian smiles at me, an ironic smile that masks a brain like a shrink's. No one's been so on-target reading my mind since my mother when I was a little kid, and I don't like it.

He cocks his head and raises one eyebrow suggestively over long lashes. If I were to sketch Adrian, I think I'd show him charming his prey. He'd have them trapped, spellbound: a siren wooing Odysseus. It's been two days since I met him, and I already know he can charm anyone, girl or guy. Turns out the guys are the only ones he's interested in.

I can't believe he's my roommate—you'd think they'd put something like that on the dorm questionnaire. I'm not sure how I feel about it, actually. I know how I *should* feel, but I don't. What does that say about me? Maybe . . . just that I don't care. I didn't come here to meet Adrian. He doesn't matter—he's only a stranger in the other half of the room. He pretends he's interested, but he doesn't know me, for all that shrink's brain of his. He sees only what the school calls me: *artist*; the way it calls him *composer*. He's already heard that no one knows what I paint. He probably thinks I'm either the next thing to hit the Museum of Modern Art or the next overrated boy wonder to hit the trash can. But what would he think if he saw my work? Maybe he'd shut off those signals, at least.

"So let's go," I tell him, sliding my sketch pad into a small backpack and slinging it over my shoulder. I keep my voice light, like I don't care one way or the other about the evening. He doesn't look like he buys it, though. If he's a composer, he probably has a fine-tuned ear. Well, he can hear what he likes. It doesn't make any difference to me.

We walk through the muggy Houston evening, hearing the screech of shadowy birds clustered in the trees above. I breathe through my mouth to avoid the pungent reek of their droppings. A migratory stop—what does that say about Whitman, as a cowbird dumping ground? We keep our pace steady and stay silent, not wanting to alarm the birds.

I could have gone to this meeting alone. But Orientation Week parties are set up by department. I went to the one for visual arts last night and saw hardly any new students from other subject areas. Adrian's music bash is tomorrow. Neither of us has an excuse for crashing the writers' party tonight. No one was checking lists last night, but I thought I'd stand out less if there were two of us from different departments. Maybe they wouldn't realize it was just me who wanted in.

Clear of the birds, Adrian leans his head back so the warm breeze ruffles his longish russet hair, this come-take-me look on his face. I glance away. Then he whistles Borodin.

I hear the lyric in my head—"Take my hand, I'm a stranger in paradise"—and have to grin. This place *is* paradise, for all of us. No more high school math and science nerds, no more worries about SATs, no more jocks, no more gangs, no more parents hanging over us, thinking they know better because they've already grown up. We have to take some regular classes, sure, but it's clear they take a backseat to our real work. Studios, practice halls, performance auditoriums—they take up more campus space than classrooms. If there's a place I might actually fit in, it could be Whitman.

Adrian glances at me and breaks off his whistling to grin back, and for a moment it's like having a friend. Then I look away.

The student center swims hazily into focus through the twilight, and I wipe my forehead, wishing I hadn't pulled on the flannel shirt.

"One word of advice, dear," Adrian murmurs. "Never let them see you sweat."

"Then I'll have to either get out of Houston or start lugging around my own air conditioner," I retort, though it's not just the outdoor temperature that's making me sweat.

Adrian wrinkles his nose. "Well, *that* would surely make you sweat."

Now we're past the cobblestone front walk and at the massive bronze doors bordered with reliefs of the muses. Corny, but also neat to see the arts taken seriously, like coming home—or more, almost like belonging. That would have been reason enough to come to Whitman, even without wanting to meet him. Or maybe they're not such different reasons.

Adrian pulls the door open grandly, and bows me into the air-conditioned front hallway reeking of lemon-scented polish. Sometimes I think he should be in the theater department. Maybe we both should. As I walk past, Adrian declaims, "Show time!" and I wince inside. How can he read me so well?

In the jumble of bodies in the main room, I can already spot the new kids—too keyed up, wary, wanting to make the right impression but not yet sure whom to impress. No—that's how they felt last night, at the visual arts get-together. And that's how they'll feel tomorrow at Adrian's music party. But tonight everyone knows whom they want to impress: Graeme Brandt.

In its own way, Whitman's reputation is just as hot as the New York High School for the Performing Arts. It's broader based, with more artistic disciplines, and it's pricier, with a gorgeous campus and private work areas for every student. Photos of the wide lawns and marble-faced concert halls and galleries are splashed across the brochures to make parents open their wallets, though there are some scholarships—enough to get me in, even as a junior transfer. But no matter how much money your parents have, it won't buy you an audition pass. I had to show my paintings to get in. Some of them, anyway. I showed four of them to audition, even though I don't let anyone see my paintings anymore. I even mortgaged myself to my parents, promising I'd study some practical subjects and make good enough grades to get into college. All because I wanted to meet Graeme Brandt.

Other schools for the arts have graduates who go on to make it big on Broadway or on the charts or in the concert halls, or even students who manage to place a story in *Harper's* or get their portfolio on file with a publisher before they graduate. But Whitman High School has Graeme Brandt. As a freshman, he wrote a young adult novel that sold and was nominated for awards in eight states its first year—Whitman had itself a real celebrity. I bought *The Eye of the Storm* through the school book club when it was first published, and I knew I had to find a way to transfer here for my last two years of high school. *To find a place to belong...*

"Charles?"

The girl's voice jars me. I didn't expect anyone to know me tonight. Careful not to show any reaction, I turn to face Rachel Holland, editor of Whitman's student journal, *Ventures.* It's a blend of literary journal and art magazine—maybe even Whitman alumni and families couldn't support two separate magazines.

"Did you think any more about what I suggested last night?" she asks.

No, I want to say. *I could care less. Now get lost.* But I can't say that to her clear brown eyes, coolly studying me, half serious, half smiling. I can't help smiling back, even though I don't want to. I see a new kid glance at her nervously; then his eyes slide away, and my own smile fades. In the middle of all the showing off and role playing, Rachel seems to be the only one who acts like she doesn't care about the masks, like she's a grown-up among kids. No—maybe it's that the rest of them are trying too hard to act grown up. It's as if she doesn't care how old she is—she just *is.* Seeing her among the other students throws me off balance, like a Dalí painting with melting clock faces. My feet seem rooted in separate, drifting worlds, and I have trouble focusing on either the crowd or the girl. How would I sketch her? Cool water, a still pool surrounded by wind-whipped flames, maybe. Or is that only what I'd *like* to see?

"Sure," I tell her. "I've thought about it." I toyed with the idea. She wants me to do sketches for *Ventures*. Actually, she wanted to know if she could print one of my paintings, but no one except the committee at auditions is going to see them. They're not the only artwork I do, though. When I told Rachel no, she didn't act surprised. She just suggested the sketches.

"When can you start?" she asks. She stands there as if she could wait for my answer forever, poised in a tailored leather vest over a soft crepe shirt—a contrast in textures that I'd like to paint.

I shrug and hook my thumb through the backpack's strap resting over my shoulder. "Maybe I'll see someone to draw tonight," I tell her. "Then you can decide if you really want my sketches."

"I do," she tells me in that odd, calm voice that sounds as though no one else is in the room with us. Can't she feel all of them hovering, hanging on the conversation so they can pass it along to anyone who's not within earshot? *Wise up,* I want to tell her. *We're all on display here—you, too.* Even though she's only a junior like me, she's been here for two years already. She should know. Maybe she does, and this cool facade is her mask. Whitman's really no different from any other school—everybody's just doing what they know they're supposed to do, being what they know they're supposed to be. Everybody except me. And Graeme Brandt.

At a swell in the voices behind me, I turn. Everyone

11

in the room turns, except Rachel—she's already facing in the right direction. A girl at a table in front of me pushes her glasses up and sighs, whispering to a friend, "It's him."

It has to be Brandt. But which one? I see a cluster of guys at the entrance. One is husky, with dark blond hair that falls over his eyes. He's laughing at something, but he doesn't look amused. He looks hungry, like a shark circling its victim. Could that be Brandt? Or is it the tall one? Slender, curly black hair, delicate hands, an incredibly beautiful face nobody'd believe on a canvas. He's telling a story, his hands moving gracefully as if he knows every eye is on him. That has to be Brandt.

He's magnetic, the kind of guy who gets voted class president and prom king and anything else he wants, just because he grabs your attention the first time you see him, and then makes you turn and look again, more closely. And when you talk to him, you feel like you've made a friend.

I half grin to myself. Kids turn to look at me twice, all right, but I can't pretend it's for the same reason. They look at me like I crawled out from under some grubby rock. It's not just because I'm short and my face is hard and bony, or because I see too much. It's probably because as soon as they see my sketches they know I'm nobody's friend. So what's the deal with Rachel and Adrian trying to get close to me so fast? Well, with Adrian I can guess, though I can't see why.

"Don't look so envious," Rachel says softly, and I hold myself motionless to keep from blinking.

"I was thinking about drawing him," I lie.

"Good," she said. "Why don't you sketch him for me? We could pair the drawing with an article on successful seniors." Her expression is perfectly calm, but I don't think she believes me.

So what? I didn't come to Whitman to meet Rachel Holland. "I'll think about it," I tell her. "But I'd have to get a better feel for him." You can't draw what you can't understand.

I circle around the tables scattered through the room, edging closer to Graeme Brandt, and can't believe Rachel's nerve. She's following me, as if we're together. Just as I'm about to tell her to get lost, she says softly, "How did you plan to meet him, just walk up and announce yourself at his grand welcome back?" She doesn't say it, but I get the message: like he'd know, or care, who Charles Weston is.

"Thanks," I say, and she smiles briefly. Well, that's fair. I could use an introduction. That doesn't mean I like her.

"Well, if it isn't play 'em Graeme," she says, raising her voice but keeping it cool. I feel the heat rising in my face—the last thing I wanted was to meet the guy by insulting him. I wish I could splash turpentine over the scene and smear it out of existence. Rachel adds, "I'm looking forward to working with you again this year."

Instead of bridling, he turns to smile at her. "Rachel! A good summer for you? Lots of revising other people's writing?"

She returns the smile. "Summer vacations are for fun. I spent the time on some writing of my own."

"A new venture," he quips, and the blond guy laughs again. "Good for you."

"I'd like you to meet a new student—Charles Weston. He'll be doing artwork for the journal. Charles—Graeme Brandt."

Too late to get out of it now. But he doesn't seem insulted by her tone. Then our eyes meet properly. His are slivers of blue ice that freeze me like a specimen before him. I can't remember being on this side of a look like that ever in my life. I slap an idiotic grin on my face and drop my head in a mock bow to duck out from the gaze. "Yeah, I've read your book." *Stupid, stupid . . .* "I guess everyone tells you that."

He laughs and nods. "Sure. But most of them haven't."

"Well, I have." This isn't going the way I expected. *But what had I thought would happen?* "What are you writing next?"

Graeme Brandt shrugs, gracefully. The guy could be a dancer. "I don't know yet. Have you got any ideas?"

The blond guy laughs hugely, and again I think of a shark. He says, "You'll take ideas from anyone, huh, Gray?"

Brandt doesn't bristle at the nickname any more than he bristled at Rachel's rhyme, just laughs along with the guy. "Anyone at all—even you, Karl. How do you think I write books *and* write for Rachel *and* turn in all my assignments on time?"

They all laugh this time, Rachel along with them. But I don't like the joke. It seems . . . cheap. Most books are junk, but his novel was something different, something that rang true for me, a warning about the games. This isn't the way I imagined him at all.

Before I can think of a way to get him to open up about his writing, an older man calls his name, and Brandt turns, his face lighting up. The man must be a teacher, perhaps Brandt's mentor? We all have one, an adult who's supposed to guide us. *Goody, goody. I can't wait to meet mine.*

Now Brandt is respectful and attentive, and even the laughing shark hangs back. I glance at Rachel. "Thanks for the intro, but don't count on a sketch anytime soon."

She watches Brandt a minute. "He's hard to see, isn't he?"

How would she know? *Play 'em Graeme...* And what does she care, anyway? I shrug. "You've just got to find the right way inside, with any subject. It's like cracking a maze, just a matter of turning around until you find your way through it."

"Good luck," she says. But there's a strangely pleased expression behind her eyes that I can't quite name. Talk about mazes to crack....

I spot Adrian standing beside sweeping bay windows, chatting to a small group, and wave in Rachel's direction as I head over to join him. This time she lets me leave.

"Charles!" Adrian beams at me and gestures to the others. "This is Wil; he writes verse. Maybe he'll do a lyric I can play with."

"Maybe you'll do some music I can write lyrics for," Wil responds good-naturedly.

"This is my new roommate, Charles," Adrian tells

them. "He paints. And this is Tyler, he writes reviews for *Ventures*. Aren't you going to sketch for them, Charles?"

Tyler snorts through a pronounced hawklike nose, and Adrian looks faintly alarmed. He goes on to name the others, but I study the reviewer. "What kind of reviews?" I ask.

He shrugs. "Any sort. I review the drama performances. I even write a music review from time to time," he says, his tone unmistakably a warning for Adrian. "I reviewed Graeme Brandt's book." He levels a killing glance across the room.

"I'm sorry I missed that," I tell him. "What did you think of it?"

"Trash," he says shortly. "Popular trash—for kids, for God's sake! He can't even write for real people, and everybody's sucking up to him."

"Have you ever had any of your own writing reviewed?" I ask.

Wil chuckles. "Rumor has it that Tyler's working on a play, but we never get to read anything he writes except reviews. Who reviews a reviewer? Other than the teachers, that is."

Tyler rounds on him. "I reviewed that poem you published in the newspaper, I believe."

Wil shuts up, and I've heard enough. I rub my head absently and look for a place to sit. Rachel wanted a sketch, and I know who to draw. Now I want somewhere to perch—a place where I can keep my back against the wall. There's an empty table midway down the room. The wall behind it is mirrored, to make the room look bigger, but as long as my back's to it I don't have to see myself. That should work fine.

I give Adrian a half smile and head for the table. *Show time.* Setting the chair against the party's reflection, I pull out my sketch pad. A couple of kids look at me with interest. I reach into the outer pocket of my backpack and take out a Waterman roller ball—even a caricature deserves a smooth line.

I uncap the pen and stretch it out like an extension of my left hand while I open the sketch pad with my right. I roll the pen through my fingers deftly, making sure the other kids can see I'm left-handed. It's supposedly no big deal, but I like to make sure people notice. My mother tried to make me color with my right hand when I was little. She said that in her day the teachers tied your left hand to your body so you had to use your right hand. That made me really eager to start school, all right.... Not that these well-trained creative people would be so crass. But as I grew up, I kind of liked seeing if I could make people notice my left-handedness—it's better than having them dislike me for myself. I hear my mother's litany: *Don't embarrass us, Charlie. We want to be proud of you—just act like everybody else when you're with them—use your right hand if they're looking—and you don't have to let them see your pictures, anyway—they make people feel uncomfortable—wait until you grow up, and then you can draw what you like.* Yeah, wait until I've given you the bragging rights to a son with a college degree so you can be proud of what I'm *not*, instead of what I am. Really good advice, Mother.

I feel a cool pair of eyes on me, and know that Rachel is watching. Well, isn't this what she wanted? And I'm keeping the real thing—*my painting*—safe. I resist the temptation to look up to see if Graeme Brandt is watching also. I close out the world and draw. I draw Tyler, exaggerating the hawk nose and sketching a frown under it that distorts his lean face into a mask of disapproval. *Those who can't do, review . . .* I pose him with a sleek fountain pen in his hand, dueling fiercely. His opponent is a mirror, reflecting the image of the critic, hacking himself to bits when he thinks he's shredding others.

As I pen the final strokes, I drift back into the room from the world of my sketch pad and hear a barely smothered snort of laughter. I sign the drawing with a quick, backward-slanted flourish and look around for Rachel Holland. I catch Tyler's furious eye and smile, daring him to take it out on a review of my work—*which he'll never see*—then pass over him.

Rachel comes to the table, and I tear off the sketch and hand it to her. "I said you might not really want my sketches," I say, no trace of apology.

She studies it, too long. "Well, I do," she says absently, and I have the feeling that she sees more than Tyler in the lines on the page. "This is a good start. Once classes begin, come by the office and we'll discuss the seniors feature."

Then she leaves, and I remember that the *Ventures* offices are in the student center, two floors up. She's taking the sketch upstairs before I can change my mind about letting her print it. Why would I take it back, though? It's a true drawing.

"Your sketches are good."

I look up. It's Graeme Brandt. Some of the other kids are watching him, but he's not the center of a mob of admiring fans anymore.

"Thanks."

"How do you see something like that in a guy?"

The way Graeme writes, the things he sees in people himself—he shouldn't have to ask. I shrug uncomfortably.

"I really don't know how to follow *The Eye of the Storm*," he tells me. "It can be hard to write a second book."

I catch an amused glint in his blue eyes. What's funny about that? It shouldn't be hard. I can see the next painting before I finish the one I'm working on. But I nod—I mean, he's trying to be friendly. That's what I wanted, isn't it? But now it doesn't seem to fit. It's like there's a wall he's built between himself and the rest of the world. I know all about walls. But when you can publish what he's written—not just see the truth, but show how you can get lost in the game—when you can write it, and get it published, and risk other people reading it and seeing inside you—*knowing you*—then why build a wall? What's left to protect? And why project this Mr. Popularity image past the wall?

I just don't get it. I stand up and slide my sketch pad inside the backpack, wishing he'd go away. A moment later, he does.

But I feel let down. Who is Graeme Brandt, if he's not the writer I imagined? Is he just the performer I saw tonight? And what will I do if he is?

2

Adrian wants to stay talking to Wil, and they're eager to welcome me into the group with congratulations on my sketch, but I've had enough. I can find my own way back to the dorm. I escape into the muggy night, my sketch pad safely zipped inside my pack. I tell myself I shouldn't be surprised at Graeme Brandt—I should know better by now.

In the front hall of my parents' home stands a glass case filled with Comedia del Arte marionettes. As a little kid, even before I started preschool, I was fascinated by them—they seemed to move around inside their cage, rearranging themselves any way they wanted. At Christmas they seemed to turn handsprings and pirouette in delight at their tiny, foil-wrapped presents. When Mother had a party, I thought the costumed figures pulled their own strings and changed places so they could greet the guests.

One Friday afternoon when I came home from kindergarten, I was stunned to see Mother home early, kneeling in front of the open case and carefully posing the marionettes in sweeping bows and graceful curtsies for a party that weekend. They were not, after all, miniature people with wills of their own, moving in answer to private desires and unspoken longings. Like all the rest of us, they performed as Mother directed.

Or as *someone* directs. It starts out—*Mother says... go to bed. Mother says... clean your room. Mother says... be a good boy—make me proud—just be yourself.* Then the rest of them. *Father says... don't cry, don't embarrass me in public. Teacher says... don't draw with your left hand, you have to learn to use your right.* Until we're all doing it. *Simon says... touch your toes. Simon says... stand on your head and give them all a good show.*

I hated playing Simon Says as a kid. I told my kindergarten teacher I didn't want to do what Simon said. I didn't want to be like Simon. I wanted to do what *I* wanted, not what Simon wanted. Mrs. Gutierrez told me I could pick which I wanted: playing Simon Says with the class or standing in the corner. No contest—I got real friendly with that corner. By first grade I could draw every crack in the chalky yellow paint.

I like laughing about it now. Laughing drowns out the truth: that there was—*is?*—something wrong with me, something more than just my being left-handed, and everybody could see it—the other kids, Mrs. Gutierrez, even my parents. Something I didn't know how to change, or how to hide. I was a slow learner. It took me until the end of middle school to figure out that life is just one big game of Simon Says, and nobody cares whether I want to do what Simon says or not. Nobody even wants to admit they're playing.

Except Graeme Brandt.

I couldn't believe it when I read *The Eye of the Storm*. He'd written about the way everyone plays games, but he wrote about a kid who understood the game, who mastered it, who never pretended to himself that he wanted anything except to win it. He acted the parts everyone wrote for him. He was the consummate Simon Says player—he knew what Simon wanted before Simon even said anything, and he was the first one doing it. He was the only one still in the circle at the end, every time. But he never played Simon's part himself.

There was a tension in the book—a sense that life was packed full of decisions that had to be made, that from moment to moment our every action was only a reaction feeding the expectations that control us in the end. The kid knew he was building his own prison, action by reaction, but what did he care? He was winning. Maybe—and I wasn't sure about this—he didn't believe that people were individuals; maybe he thought they were just carbon copies that made a community, the way all the houses in a subdivision have the same floor plan even if they're disguised with different-colored aluminum sidings.

I read *The Eye of the Storm* as a warning story, like the old Aesop's fables—only the other kids never got it. Everybody was reading the book at my old school, but they never saw that. How could they miss it? I was so sure Graeme Brandt was showing everybody how ter-

22

rible the game could be, so they'd realize and stop playing it. But after seeing him, it's as if he's just playing the game, too. If he is, then how could he write about it so honestly?

Nobody talks about the game—maybe they can't even admit to themselves that it exists. Only outsiders like me, who won't play, seem to see it. That's why I was so sure Graeme had to be like me, only better, because he could use his art to expose the game, to warn people about it and not be destroyed by them. Maybe that's still true. It was only a party, after all. I was just expecting (*wanting*) him to be different.

I pause at the tree line and listen to the rustling leaves and birds perched above, a low murmur punctuated by sudden raucous cries that are answered by creaks and shifts in the tree branches and new rustlings. Then I stretch my stride and make my footfalls soft, cat-like, on the pavement. I barely breathe. The thought of alarming hundreds of cowbirds is powerful inspiration to stay silent. How would I sketch the scene? A huddled figure, straining for the open green lawn ahead, only to step on a dry, weathered twig that cracks ominously. The figure darts a panic-stricken look above to see a cloud of feathered wings rise from the shuddering treetops.

That's what I'd draw for *Ventures*—the *reality*, but not the *possibility* that I'd paint for myself.

I reach the dorm safely and hide out in our room. It still looks...I don't know, undefined—a scattering of Adrian's clothes and music notebooks in closets and on shelves along one side of the room, and a CD player and headphones on his desk, CDs stacked in the shelves intended for textbooks. He's already at home.

The policy at Whitman is for new students to room with somebody who's already been here at least a year. For freshmen, that means rooming with a sophomore. For junior transfers like me, it's usually someone in the same grade. They say it's to keep us from getting too homesick, to help us fit into boarding-school life. It's probably to keep us from bugging our mentor with too many questions on how things are supposed to run—the roommate knows the rules. *Adrian says . . . go to class. Adrian says . . . show time.*

There's nothing on my side of the room except clothes in the closet and a few empty sketch pads and blank notebooks for classes on my desk, along with a large hasp lock and a scattering of roller ball refills for my pen, a computer I didn't want, and a file folder with a copy of my application to Whitman. I pick that up and open it. They wanted a biographical sketch to round out their form. A *sketch . . .*

I drew them a sketch, of course: a self-portrait from the back, me standing before an easel. They couldn't see my face because it's turned away from them, and they couldn't see my painting because the canvas remained white. I hadn't yet begun. All you could see were the possibilities.

My parents said that wasn't enough. If I seriously wanted to get into this school, they said I had to *write* a biographical sketch, because that was what the instructions obviously meant. *Obvious to whom?* But I did want to get in, so I wrote it:

I was born with a crayon in one hand and a stick of colored chalk in the other. At least, from the way my mother complains of the mess I made drawing before I started school, I must have been. By the time I began preschool I was working in chalks, as they were easiest to clean up. I moved on to poster paints in preschool and was soon experimenting with different tools: the finger versus the brush.

I painted packs of wolves chasing indistinct figures in preschool and kindergarten. The grown-ups said the pictures were very nice, but clearly they didn't like the savage quality of the wolves. The other kids thought the wolves were cool, but they didn't like the fact that my drawings of wolves actually looked like wolves instead of like black stick figures with big teeth—or maybe they didn't like the fact that I couldn't help laughing at their awkward stick figures. Take your pick. So what if they were better at kicking a ball or playing catch than I was? That didn't stop them from laughing at me when the teacher forced me to play their games at recess—or from resenting that I was better with paint. It didn't stop them from calling me names, although the teachers finally stopped them from calling me colored boy (I *did* seem to end up with almost as much paint on me as on the paper).

The kids understood instinctively that the wolf pack was the whole bunch of them, mediocrity incarnate, chasing the one who was different. None of us had the words for it then, of course, but I had the imagery, and the talent, to show it. What I wanted was someone to see my paintings and nod and say, "That's how it is, all right." But no one did, not even the teachers or parents. Maybe they were scared of admitting they were part of the wolf pack, even to themselves. Maybe they wished they could be different, special—the one who escaped the wolves. But they couldn't be, or they just wouldn't try.

I began sketching people in first grade.

Miss Bush, my first-grade teacher, took away my sketch pad and told me to concentrate on reading and addition and subtraction, so I drew on the ruled pages of my workbook and in the margins of the schoolbooks. I sketched Miss Bush drawing big red *X*s over students who didn't pay attention. She found my drawings when she graded our workbooks and was furious—and hurt. How did she think *I* felt when she told me I was "wasting my time" drawing "stupid" pictures in class? I was glad I could make her hurt back.

After that, she even said my paintings in art were wrong. How can a painting be wrong, unless it's a lie? She told us to paint flowers, and I painted a meadow of wildflowers, bright colors dancing above the weeds, a deer looking up as it ate a flower. "Wrong!" Miss Bush told me. "This is a flower!" And right on top of my meadow she drew an ugly daisy with a black Magic Marker. Sure, she'd drawn a daisy on the chalkboard when she told us to draw flowers, but I didn't think she actually meant us to *copy* it. When I looked around me, however, the other kids all had rows of identical daisies on their drawing paper. Well, if they all thought they were supposed to copy her model, okay for them. But telling us to paint flowers didn't sound anything like saying "reproduce daisy clones"—at least not to me. Why should I draw them that way?

In second grade I was put in charge of the artwork for the class bulletin board and the backdrops for our class play.

Second grade was worse, because Mrs. Argenta actually seemed to like my drawings at first. She asked me to do the bulletin board artwork. "See how Charlie painted the tree trunk on the backdrop, boys and girls? Now you paint more trees just like his." But the other kids couldn't, and they resented me. I realized after a while that Mrs. Argenta didn't really *see* what I painted—she only saw that I could draw and paint. She couldn't teach art, so she told the other kids to copy me. Maybe she expected me to teach them. But I didn't know how. Anyway, you can't just copy something. You have to make it your own somehow, and paint that. Mrs. Argenta got impatient with the other kids and mad at me for not showing them how to do what I did. I finally sketched her blind, with dark glasses and a cane, holding up a large brush that was really a puppeteer's stick, with the strings attached to brushes the other students were holding. After that Mrs. Argenta didn't make me show the class how to draw anything anymore, but the kids never forgot I'd said it was a waste of time trying to show them how to paint the way I did.

The names got worse, and I started zipping my sketch pad inside a backpack to keep it safe. Paintings I did in art stopped making it to the bulletin board. Somehow they ended up on the bottom of the pile, and sometimes they ended up torn. The reports of "Doesn't play well with others" and "Doesn't follow instructions" started to bother my parents. They had a parent-teacher conference, but Dad came home saying Mrs. Argenta was a flake, so nothing happened. I wasn't sure, however, that she was all that different from the rest of them.

The following summer I began working in watercolors and experimenting with textures.

I found I could achieve a luminous quality with watercolors, especially when I textured them by painting over pencil work. I could have lived in my room forever, drawing and painting, if only I'd had someone to share it with. I showed Mom, and she said my pictures were "very nice," but she wanted me to get out and play. I noticed she didn't really look at the pictures anymore. Maybe she'd figured out she was just another wolf in the pack (even though I wasn't painting wolves anymore) and didn't like the feeling.

But that's not what I wanted. I wanted people to look at my paintings and think, "Yes, I could be the one standing out—I could be different from the rest—I *am* different from the rest—there's something special about me." Why didn't anybody see that? Other kids acted like they wanted to be special, so I couldn't understand why my being different made them dislike me. Wasn't I only doing what they wanted to do?

By third grade I had gained a reputation among my peers as a caricature artist, sketching various teachers and classmates.

Third grade was torture, with a teacher who thought art was a waste of time, even in art class. Mr. Birkin told the rest of the class that I was a "distraction," a "trouble-maker," "too self-absorbed." He moved me to the far back corner of the classroom and made comments like, "Do tell us if the history lesson disturbs you, young van Gogh." Then he told the class how van Gogh was crazy. I drew Mr. Birkin again and again in my sketch pad as a crippled, hunched-over skeleton clawing through paintings that clung to the wall, despite their tatters. I tried not to listen to him, which made it hard to pass third grade. Mr. Birkin was going to keep me back, but my parents mobilized to prevent that. They made the school test me, proving that I actually could read and do math, even if my grasp of history and science was rather vague.

When I left Mr. Birkin's classroom for the last time, I put a drawing on his desk that showed him torturing a jail cell full of students—whips and chains and all kinds of things I'd seen in an old black-and-white movie on cable. From the hallway I could hear the sound of paper ripping.

In fourth grade I began incorporating classical symbolism into my paintings. By this time I was working in watercolors, pen-and-ink, charcoal, colored pencils, or colored chalk, depending on the project.

It was fourth grade that taught me that school actually could be useful. I made sure to do my homework and study for tests, but I didn't always listen in class. One afternoon, though, Ms. Geller was talking about mythology, and she told us the story of the phoenix rising from its ashes. It suddenly occurred to me that I could use a reference like that in my paintings. If you painted a symbol that everybody recognized, then it could help them understand what the painting meant.

I got really excited by the idea and painted the phoenix in the next art class—I added in lions, their tawny bodies contrasting with the gold of the phoenix's feathers as they tore it apart, only to have it burst into flames in their claws and rise above them, reborn. I thought Ms. Geller would love it since I used what she'd said in class, but she looked uncomfortable and said it was "striking." She said I was "very talented." She put it on the bottom of the pile of drawings. Maybe she didn't like the lions tearing the phoenix apart. But what does she think it feels like, having everybody telling you you're strange, you're different, you don't go along with the crowd, you don't play what we like to play, you don't think what we think, *what's wrong with you?* As if it never occurs to them that there might be something wrong with them. It *feels* like claws ripping you to pieces. And if you don't believe you can rise from the fire, then you'll just shrivel up and die inside.

In fifth grade the kids were banding together into clubs (*packs*), some sanctioned by the school, some overlooked. The kids who'd called me the worst names started flashing a hand signal at each other. Mrs. Silverman was teaching us sign language in English class, and I recognized the letter "K" repeated three times fast, but I didn't know what they meant, and didn't care; at least until I saw it on one kid's notebook. "KKK" and beneath it "Klu Klux Kharles." Someone had been doing their American history homework, even if the alliteration was a little strained. My locker door got slammed a lot that year, just as I was trying to reach inside it. And my homework never made it to Mrs. Silverman in one piece unless she walked up and down the aisles, picking up everyone's paper herself. I painted sweeping heraldic birds and threatening forests in art class, and wasn't surprised when a jar of rinse water or another kid's pot of paint splashed over my paper. Mrs. Silverman knew I was a loner and tried to be encouraging, but either she never guessed about the Klu Klux Kharles or she thought it must be innocuous. It's not as if any fighting went on in her class. What was the point of fighting with fists if paint couldn't make them see?

By seventh grade I was working in oils, combining modern symbols with classical references for different effects. I also contributed cartoons to the school newspaper.

31

In middle school, art was an elective. I took it more to get out of wood or metal shop than to learn anything about art. At home I was painting in oils, using their richness to capture unicorns hunted by men with barking dogs, and stags bounding away from wolves. But I was getting more interested in modern symbols: city buildings and streetlights—architecture that defied gravity, and light that defied nature. I was saying—shouting!—in my paintings: *Look what we have done! Look what you can do! Reach for what you can be!* But reaching meant standing alone, balancing unsteadily, straining for a star high above you—and I guess to most people that meant falling.

Ms. D'Abati, my seventh-grade art teacher, must have thought so—she gave me a C for a painting of a figure balanced on a shuddering branch, one arm extended toward a light that silhouetted the figure's outstretched hand like a radiant halo crowning the future. Ms. D'Abati told me the figure was out of proportion—the hand was too large and the head was too small. The balance of figure on branch was improbable. The contrast between light and dark was too great. She probably would never have believed angels could dance on the head of a pin, either. It hurt. I hated myself for letting it hurt, but it did. It always surprised me when I showed someone a painting and they tore it apart—literally, or with a grade. It was as if they were saying, "Don't tell me I have to aim so high. I don't want to hear it." And they'd want to shred the message bearer (*or the artist*) as well as the message.

In eighth grade I thought things were changing when

I started hanging out with Steve. He didn't paint, but he was into videos—he'd film them, then edit them on his computer. We both had Mrs. Sayers for art class, and she actually seemed to like art. She let Steve show one of his videos for a special project, and I could see he really loved playing with the camera. I told him it was great, and he seemed pleased. I thought he'd understand my art (*I thought he was like me*). But Steve was always busy—he played soccer, he sat around the pizza place with the other kids, he hung out in video arcades, and he said he spent more time playing games on his computer than video-editing. He'd tell me to come on with the rest of the gang, even though the others didn't like me. I thought it was a waste of time, frankly. Why not be painting, instead? Why didn't Steve want to spend the time on his videos?

I finally showed Steve some of my paintings, things no one in school had seen. He was blown away—I could see that. And I thought, *Well, at last!* He told me, "Man—these are good!" Then he got quiet, and seemed kind of uncomfortable. I asked him why, but he just shrugged and said again how good they were. Which would have been okay, except that he kind of avoided me after that. I told myself to just forget about him, but I couldn't. I'd really thought we could be friends. So I finally cornered him after school one day and just asked: *Why?* Of course he knew what I meant. He told me, "They're really good ... but ... it's like they ask too much. I can't really explain it, but looking at your pictures, I feel like I ought to be different than I am, somehow— trying to do the impossible. Is that what you want people to think?" When I told him not really (I hardly knew how to answer), he said, "I mean, they make me feel like what I do is a waste of time, and I don't like that feeling. I like who I am. I don't like feeling like I'm not measuring up." Then he asked, "So, you want to come hang out or what?" I shook my head. And that was the end of being friends with Steve.

My grades remained respectable during this period, but it was clear that public school could not provide adequate art instruction, such as what I would hope to receive at Whitman.

My biographical sketch: pompous, entirely truthful, and utterly unrevealing. But Whitman's audition committee must have bought it—they took me. I drop the file folder and turn away from the desk. I sit on my unmade bed and pull out the sketch pad I used for Tyler, then uncap my pen and let it wander. I expect to see the bird-filled trees emerge, but instead the lines take on the contour of Graeme Brandt's head. I stare at the shape. How would I draw him for Rachel? I could give her a photographic image without ever cracking the maze, but that's not what I do. If I draw him, I have to expose him, the way I get inside everybody else. I thought I'd find treasure inside Graeme Brandt. I mean, he's another teen, like me. He's had to have had other kids and teachers tear him down. And he's had to have seen them living Simon Says, in order to write about it.

But he got his book published and he put it out there for everyone to read—so he must not care if they tear him down. He must be confident enough to show himself in his art and not care, or at least not be hurt by the way people react. *Admit it, you thought you'd find someone who knew the secret, who could show you how to get beyond the game, someone who could show you how to have it both ways—how to be who you are, and how to paint what you have inside you and be able to show everyone, the way he did with that book. Surely it made people uncomfortable when they saw themselves in it. And yet they read it. I hide my paintings away to keep them from being shredded, and yet they're crying to be seen. I thought he could show me how to do it—I thought he could show me how to keep from locking myself away inside a studio forever. That can't be the way life is supposed to be lived.*

I thought he could be a friend. Stupid, stupid.

But whatever he is inside, why can't I find the way in? He's public property—his soul should be an open book, the way Tyler's is. It's as if the Graeme Brandt I saw tonight was a different person than the Graeme Brandt who wrote that book. The image of Janus, two-faced, springs to mind. I see two faces, one turned to his computer keyboard and one turned to his readers. But I shake off the idea. It's too much like my own defense mechanism, and that's what I want an escape from. Graeme's got to be more than that.

I slam the sketch pad shut and shove it back inside my pack. Now that I've met him, I want to forget him. I want it to be tomorrow already—I want to get through the meeting with Mr. Brooks, my mentor, find my studio, and unpack my supplies. This dorm room is just for show—the studio will be for *me,* where no one will laugh at my paintings or, worse, look from them to me and then edge away from me, wishing they hadn't seen the paintings, wishing they hadn't seen inside of me, wishing they didn't know me. *Someday, I'll have an apartment all my own, a short hallway between studio and home, a cave to hide out in that I never have to leave.* It's a familiar wish—more than a wish, maybe a plan (*even though I know it's a plan for a half life and I still dream of finding a way to live a full life*). For now, though, I pick up the lock and sling its comforting weight around my forefinger. Locking the studio had better not be a problem.

I want to paint the birds in the trees, waiting for a victim—but a victim who will surprise them.

Excerpts from
Graeme Brandt's Journal

August 29 (Senior Year)

I can't think how else to start this year's journal. Senior year, and one real, *published* book already. I should be flying high. Whitman never had a writer who's actually published a book before graduation—not until me. Mr. Adler's bursting with pride that I'm his protégé. Which is kind of interesting, since he's never published anything himself. But the school named him my mentor when I started, so he gets credit for guiding me in the right direction. The only question now is: What direction is that?

I should be laying out plans for the book I'm going to write this year. It used to be so easy to start writing. I've never been at a loss for an idea before: short stories, my first book. But looking back at them, they all seem to tell the same story—or at least express the same idea. I want to write something new—but I don't seem to have any new ideas in my head.

I could coast. I could sit back and say I'm working, or I'm thinking. I could accept everybody's praise, and I'd still graduate a hit. I've earned it. But . . . I *care* about my writing. And I don't want to accept that the one book is all I see, all I believe, all I can write. When I started it, I knew instinctively what I wanted to say. Did I say it all? Have I been here three years since writing the first page of it and not learned anything else to write along the way?

I was taught that a writer expresses for his readers the world as he sees it. He should write what he knows, from his experience of the world, and show his readers what they can't understand for themselves. Well, I wrote what I knew, and my book *is* true. I only have to look in the eyes of the teachers who read it. I only have to test it with my own friends, and I see that I showed my world honestly. But I keep having the sense that there's something else out there—some mystery I don't understand yet. And it's not just a matter of growing up—it's something I can see in the rapt faces of other students here at Whitman as they lose themselves in the act of creating something—even Karl, when he's lost in his sculpture. He hasn't actually read my book, just heard about it, and he's certainly no tower of intellect, but he seems to know something I don't know. I see him focus on his sculpture, and I feel left out, as if I'm not there at all, as if I don't exist.

Or is that all in my imagination? Maybe so—but that doesn't explain the empty space I feel growing inside myself every year that I work harder and harder at my writing, instead of just being an ordinary teenager, my parents' son, or my teachers' student. I feel as if I'm reaching for words to express something I should understand intuitively. But I strain and grasp, and my hand, my heart, my soul closes on emptiness, on wisps of truth, on nothing.

What if I'm not really cut out to be a writer at all?

I can't imagine myself working in a factory production line, or an office, or a store—or doing anything except writing. Everybody's always expected me to be a writer—that's what I'm supposed to be. I'm sure I could imagine myself into some other job, like I imagine my characters into roles, but everyone would be so disappointed in me. Yet, all summer, and even now, I find myself lying awake nights, thinking, and trying to think, but nothing comes. I sit down at my computer, and too soon my neck burns from hunching my shoulders and my fingers feel stiff. It's ninety degrees out, and probably 90 percent humidity, and I'm cold all the time. Sometimes my eyes blur and things fade to the point I can barely read, and my head pounds and I feel like screaming. I don't know what's happening to me.

I look at my book, at my life. What do I do now? If only I could see what the other students see, the mystery that would fill the empty space inside of me, what they instinctively know that I can't understand. That's what I have to uncover—for my readers and for myself. Then I'll know what to write.

So I'm going to do something different with this journal. I'm going to keep it on CD for a start, so no one can ever read it on my hard drive. And it's not the one I'll be handing in to Mrs. Roberts. Usually I start a story with a theme and character descriptions and a plot outline, and I'll conjure up that stuff for her later on. But here I'm going to start with me. I've got diaries from when I was a kid. I've got files—stories I started to write that just ran out of steam, journal entries, and notes on scraps of paper mixed in with pages from other manuscripts. I'm going to sift through all this, put the ones that seem most significant on this disc, and try to find a pattern that goes beyond the first book. There's got to be something.

What will come from this, I can't guess. But it scares me—the kind of scary you feel when you're six and you see *Frankenstein* for the first time, and you're horrified and sorry for the monster and sick with dread all at once. That wears

39

off gradually as you grow up, until you can watch the ax-wielding undead come after the hero in part twenty-six of a never-ending series and barely feel a shiver.

Well, rolling back the years was what I wanted to do, after all. I'm that kid again, scared and thrilled and feeling a little sick inside, but not wanting anybody to know. There aren't any easy answers waiting in happy memories. There isn't any surface stuff I can get away with writing about. I've got to look within, until I find something that I, and only I, can see and express—something that I haven't said before. Maybe something that no one has said before.

MEMORY LANE

November 10 (Third Grade)

Mom gave me this notebook. It says "Graeme's Book" on the cover. She wrote it for me in cool letters—*calligraphy,* she calls it. My letters are messy, even if they say good stuff. At least my teacher, Mrs. Ferris, says I write good. So Mom said I was going to be a writer, and she got me this book. She says to write down all my thoughts and everything I do. I'm supposed to write in it every day.

I wonder what being a writer is like. I wrote a story about a black dog who finds a kid who needs a dog, and Mrs. Ferris said it's the best story any of her third graders ever wrote. That was fun. Maybe it's fun making up stories and getting paid for it.

Not all the other kids thought it was fun when they heard Mrs. Ferris say that, though. Ali and Ryan were mad she didn't think their stories were the best. But I told them I didn't care. I said I didn't think writing mattered. Playing kickball was more fun. I said that because Ryan's really good at kickball. Then they weren't so mad at me anymore. But I really think both writing and kickball are fun.

It's hard to think what to write in here. I know—I was playing kickball with Mike and he missed and I called him fumble foot and he hit me. My nose hurt.

Maybe I shouldn't write that in here, in case Mom's going to read it.

But I figured out why he did it. He didn't care about the name. He cared because other kids heard at recess. I can call him names when we're alone and he doesn't mind. He even likes some of the names I come up with. But I'll remember not to do it where other kids can hear, so I don't get punched again.

It's getting late. I have to figure out what to write down in this book, and what to keep in my head. It's hard work being a writer.

August 21 (Fourth Grade)

First day of school, and I wanted to tell Mom about my new teacher. I got a man this year! Too cool. But Dad was home early—weird. And he was really mad. He and Mom went to their room and talked forever. Dinner was late.

There was some account that Dad was supposed to get at the bank, but something went wrong and the account went to City National, instead. That's a bigger bank than the one where Dad works, but Mom always says Dad's too good for City National. I don't know what she means. Dad beams when she says it, though, so I guess it must be true.

Anyway, my stomach was growling. I was about to beat on the door and beg for food, but then I started listening. Last year Mrs. Ferris told me to practice writing conversations, but I never heard anything interesting to write down. Trading insults with Mike didn't seem like enough.

But this time, it was like I was hearing Mom and Dad for the first time. I couldn't see their faces, just hear their voices. Mom's voice was all soft and comforting, but Dad's was harsh and kind of scary. So I sat in the hall and listened, and I'm going to try to write it down the way I remember it.

"Why did Mr. Harris go to City National, Andy? That's so silly." Mom sounded helpless and understanding at the same time. She sounds that way sometimes, but only with Dad. Never with me.

"No, it's not. They have more branches and more of a reputation." Now Dad didn't sound so angry, just tired. He gave a little laugh. "Reputation! Sure didn't do much for mine. We can kiss that promotion good-bye."

I got a little spooked at that. Would not getting that promotion mean that things might change at home? And it was funny listening to Dad talk like that. He never says things like "kiss it good-bye" to me. They're different together than they are when I'm around.

"Well, you've got lots of other accounts," Mom told him. Her voice was so low I could hardly make it out.

"Sure. They'll look at my track record—I can still bring in plenty of accounts without Jim Harris. I'll get that promotion yet." Now Dad sounded almost happy. The account was still lost, but he sounded like he didn't care so much anymore.

"Of course you will."

Mom's voice was so soft it blurred, and Dad laughed and

his voice got low and kind of thick, and I couldn't understand him anymore. I felt sort of strange, so I went back to my room. When Mom came out, she made pork chops and twice-baked potatoes, so dinner was okay. And Dad was in a good mood. We watched a cool science fiction movie on cable, and he just laughed at the weird aliens. Usually he changes the channel.

December 4 (Fifth Grade)

Football on TV, and I've got my book hidden in my school binder so I can write. Dad's cheering for the Redskins, but I can't get excited unless it's baseball.

Mom said I should work on settings—describing rooms and houses and places for my stories. She said it's important for the reader to be able to see the setting so he feels like he's in the book. Makes me feel like a magician, casting a spell and pulling somebody out of their reading chair into my story.

Okay—so, my room at home. It isn't too big, but it's all mine. I can shut the door and pretend it's my own private world—until Mom comes in, that is. Actually, I don't shut the door much. Walls—painted pale blue. And I've got pictures of baseball players taped up everywhere. My bed's pushed into a corner so I have more room on the floor. There's a blue-and-white bedspread tangled up somewhere on the bed, but I don't see it too often because I pile up sweatshirts and games and junk on top.

That gives me more room on the floor—polished wood, not so waxed that I skid on it. I've got an army of plastic knights set up in one corner of the room. But there's an ambush of infidels waiting behind my closet door (painted blue, too—the door, not the infidels!). They'll leap out and slaughter the band of noble knights any minute. I've stationed a troop of armored cavalry beside my dresser, though, so reinforcements are on the way.

I know—eleven is too old to play with toy soldiers. And I've got some excellent battle video games. But I still think it's more fun to lie on the floor, moving the knights around, than it is pushing some joystick. I'll probably put them away next year. I shove them under the bed if Mike or the other guys come over to visit.

What else? There's a desk, of course—like polished wood, only it's really pressboard with some sort of veneer. It came in pieces and Dad had to assemble it—he muttered a lot of stuff under his breath until Mom said it was the best they could afford. Then he kept quiet, even when the screwdriver dug into the pressboard, skittered off, and gouged his hand. I can still feel the uneven rut along the inside corner. I've got the desk placed under the window, so I can see outside when I sit there. Not much to see—trees, and a neighbor's yard through the leaves. In the winter I can see the sky. I like it when it storms and the sky gets dark. It looks like clouds of black ash you could drown in.

On the desk are piles of papers and books. Mom groans, but I know where all my junk is. And I can shove everything onto the bed if I need more space to write. There's a cold, bright white lamp there, not at all like the soft yellow light in the ceiling. When I sit at my desk under that cold light, I feel like I'm in some sort of a writing office, just like Dad's office at the bank. It makes me think really seriously about the sorts of things I want to write. What I like about reading a good story is that it makes me think about ideas I hadn't thought about before—I don't always agree with what the writer says, or what the teacher says about the ideas, but it makes me think about them. That's what I'm going to do in my stories: Make my readers think about ideas.

I spend some time at my writing job every night, which thrills Mom. "My son, the writer," she says. And she shakes her head and smiles. Dad rolls his eyes, but he smiles, too.

December 5 (Fifth Grade)

The Redskins were way behind at halftime and Dad got really mad, so I hid my book and went up to bed. I was lying there in the dark, thinking about having a writing office, and a real writing job, and I wanted to write about that before I go to school.

Am I a real writer? Am I going to write stories, and maybe even books, for the rest of my life? Maybe. I mean—I guess I am. Sometimes, though, I wonder what it would be like to be a professional baseball player. I said that once to Mom, and she laughed. So I got mad and said I really meant it. I shouldn't have done that! Mom really blew her stack. "Don't say that," she yelled at me. "I didn't sacrifice everything so my son would turn out a ballplayer!"

I don't like it when she talks like that. She dropped out of college because of me, and she says it's all right because I'll do everything she didn't do. I'll be a famous writer, and I'll make it all worthwhile for her. I should have shut up when she started to talk about everything she'd sacrificed, but I was thinking how good the leather in my mitt smelled after I oiled it, and how great it felt to stretch for the ball, one toe on the base, knowing it was going to be close but still knowing I'd get the runner out and everybody would cheer. So I said something dumb like, "But I *want* to be a baseball player."

She grabbed the TV remote and threw it across the room at me. I ducked and it hit the wall behind me, so she grabbed a box of tissues and threw them at me, too. Then she started to cry. And she didn't have any tissues. So I picked up the box (the corner was kind of smashed in, but the tissues were okay) and brought it back to her. Then I went to get the remote. The battery compartment had come open when it hit the wall, so I had to crawl around on the floor for the batteries. And Mom's saying, "I'm sorry, I'm sorry—but you're such a good writer, Graeme, and you like writing, don't you? Don't you really? And the doctor said you have a heart murmur—you can't be a professional athlete with a heart murmur! Be honest, Graeme—don't you like writing better than baseball?"

What could I say? There was no point in trying to remind her that the doctor said I could play ball, that it was even good for my heart. She needed to hear me say yes, she really did. And I do like writing. I really like it a lot. So I said, "Sure, Mom. Sure I do."

March 16 (Seventh Grade)

Mom said I should practice character descriptions. She told me that every novel needs characters that the reader can believe in, and that makes sense to me—the characters are the ones who have the ideas that make the reader think, after all. She said I should practice describing my friends at school, so here goes.

My best friend is Michael Raynor. He's been my best

friend since he moved here in second grade. We used to fight when we were little kids, and we still do, but we're totally close. Mike's the captain of our baseball team, and he's the best pitcher we have. I play second base, and we've got the timing down for awesome double plays. It's a fun sport, but I probably won't keep playing in high school. Ballplayers there are thinking about playing baseball in college, maybe even going on to the minors, and I'm not that serious. It's just a game, just for fun.

I guess I haven't really shown a reader much about Mike, have I? Well, he's taller than me, and he's got brown hair that he wears kind of long, with a braided pigtail in the back, and he's got these big brown eyes. He sings in the school choir, like me, but his voice is starting to break and that bugs him a lot. He's easygoing about most things, though, and he's pretty smart, especially about animals. His dad takes him hunting, and he knows all about different kinds of animals and where to find them. I went with them once, but I decided I didn't really like it, and Mom was horrified at the thought of me going hunting. I can't tell whether Mike likes it himself, or if he just says he does because his dad likes it. He probably likes being with his dad all alone, without his mom or his sister around.

Mike doesn't like school much, even though he's smart. He'd rather play baseball or soccer. He's a terrific pitcher, but he's not so great at kicking the ball. I don't say anything, though, just go to his soccer games and cheer. And I don't tell him I like school pretty well myself. He'd just think I was weird, and I like playing baseball with him okay. Anyway, it's not important. The way to keep a friend is by just doing what they want—I mean, as long as it doesn't really matter.

School—yeah, I like it. Actually, I like the teachers more than the other kids, mostly anyway. My homeroom teacher this year is Mr. Lester, and he talks to me about all sorts of stuff. He was trying to teach me how to speed-read the other day, and that was pretty interesting. I didn't really want to learn (actually, I like reading every word in a book and getting totally involved in the story), but I didn't want to hurt his feelings. He's old, with thinning gray hair. But he's got these bright blue eyes, and he's really smart. We talk about all kinds of things, stuff that doesn't have anything to do with school. He's married, but he's only got daughters. Maybe he likes talking to a boy sometimes.

Then there's this one English teacher, Mr. Shaw. All the kids jump all over him, but I kind of like him. I go in to talk to him during lunch period sometimes. I think he's scared to eat in the cafeteria. He tells me about Shakespeare, because I told him I liked Shakespeare. What's a guy who likes Shakespeare doing teaching middle school, anyway? He should be in a college somewhere, where it's safe. He's about twenty-five, I guess, with blond hair and hazel-green eyes, and he wears glasses and looks spooked most of the time—I guess because he knows the kids trash him behind his back. But he's got a nice-looking face when he relaxes, and he smiles at me whenever he sees me in the hall. I almost wish he was my English teacher—except I wouldn't want to let on that I liked him in front of everybody else.

It's easier when you're one-on-one with someone. You can see what they're like, and what they expect of you. That makes things easier than being with a bunch of people who are all different. Maybe I should practice writing about crowds, like the guys on the baseball team, or the whole choir, or the whole seventh grade at assembly!

But that's all I have time to write now. I like describing people I know. It's like looking through a window to see what someone's doing when he doesn't know you're looking. And I can do it by just sitting back and seeing inside my own head.

3

"You'll find things here different than what you're accustomed to, Charles," Mr. Brooks tells me. "More structured."

He smiles patiently. Acting laid-back in jeans and a baggy sweater (despite the sticky heat outside, his office is a deep-freeze), he's the perfect image of the wise and kindly older mentor who will guide young talent to success.

"Your audition paintings were most impressive, but you still have an undisciplined approach. Very undisciplined. This often happens with artists who are self-taught—the talent and inspiration are there, but adequate training in the fundamentals is lacking. As you're a junior"—he shakes his balding head regretfully—"you'll be taking some advanced classes, of course. But I really think you'd benefit from some basics." When I don't say anything, he elaborates. "I'd like you to take Still Life, to give you precision, and Anatomy and Modeling, to give your human figures greater accuracy and better proportion."

He glances at me across his sleek black desk slab, but I keep my mouth shut. He can put me down for any classes he likes, even introductory finger painting, if he'll just tell me where my studio is. Despite what I wrote in my application, I didn't come to Whitman expecting to be taught anything about painting. I thought Graeme Brandt was the only instructor I needed, but I expected him to teach me how to *show* my art, not how to do it better.

"Your composition is sound," he allows. "For the advanced classes, I'd suggest Portraiture, and Landscape. How does that sound?"

I resist the shrug that's itching to burst out, and nod. "Fine." If the landscapes hanging on his paneled walls are any example of what the advanced class teaches, I'll learn what *not* to do.

"You'll also be taking Junior English, Government, French— I don't see any math or science on your preference sheet—"

"I've done calculus and chemistry," I tell him. "That's more math and science than I'll probably ever need. It's on my transcript."

"Oh." He flips the page, and his eyes light up. "I see you wanted some computer programming?"

This time I do shrug. *Thanks for coming up with that idea, Dad. Learn to paint on a computer and see the world . . .* "I was thinking about doing some sort of computer graphics," I explain reluctantly. "Sort of a way to make a living, maybe."

"Good thinking," he says, pushing up the loose sleeves on his sweater. "But you can't really fly before you can swim." He chuckles, I guess at his hopelessly mixed metaphors. "I'll put you down for Introductory Programming. Then you'll be ready to program graphics next year."

I take the schedule he hands me and note that Gym is a bare thirty minutes twice a week. The computer class is an hour three days, which seems like a lot of wasted time. Maybe I can learn to write a program that will give me a passing grade in the course without having to actually attend it. The mornings are full of academic courses, but the afternoons are all art classes and studio time.

"Now," Mr. Brooks says in a portentous tone, "for your studio."

I slide the schedule into my jeans pocket and wait. He opens a soundless drawer in his desk and pulls out a brass key and a sheet of paper. "Usually upperclassmen get to choose their studios in the spring, but as you're a transfer we selected one for you from what was left."

The sheet of paper is a floor plan of the studio building, and I watch as his finger hovers over it. "This one is all the way at the far end, I'm afraid, but it does have the advantage of being near the elevators, which made it easier to get your materials inside."

I ignore his disapproving tone. I crated my paintings myself so no one could see them, but it all weighed a ton in the end. I had to send them by slow truck, and it still ate up most of my savings account.

The studio he's pointing to looks perfect. Squashed in a corner between a stairwell and the bank of elevators, it's odd-shaped—narrower at the door, with a dogleg corner jutting into the floor space. That's probably why no one else wanted it. But it's isolated, which suits me fine.

"Even though it's a little smaller than the others, you've got a good north light," Mr. Brooks is saying. "And you'll have the opportunity to choose a different studio for your senior year, of course."

"This one's okay." I just want to get out of his office and into my studio.

He hands me the key. "This will get you into the building and into your studio itself. But I'm afraid these keys aren't impossible to copy. To keep your materials safe, you should probably get an additional lock."

Already done. The weight of the hasp lock dragged awkwardly in my pack on the way here. I take the floor plan and key and start to stand up.

"We're very pleased to have you as part of the Whitman family, Charles," Mr. Brooks intones, and I sink back into my chair. Family? Who's he kidding? One reason most kids are here is wanting to get away from family—parents who start out proud because Junior plays the violin and then think he's weird when he finds out he's really good and starts to get obsessed. *Simon says... get out and play, be like the other kids—what's wrong with you?* Here, there's nothing wrong with us.

I think of my father looking flushed and hurt when I didn't care who was winning the stupid football game— all I wanted to do was paint the receiver, hanging in midair, his fingertips brushing the rough, pebbly texture of the ball. He knows that three guys, each one twice his size, are about to crash into him, but he makes himself tune them out, straining to clasp that ball to his chest and bring it to earth with him. Except for the colors of the uniforms on canvas, the teams' identities don't matter. I intended to paint red and gold for the receiver, to echo the autumn crispness, but I wanted to give Dad the painting. *Stupid idea—but part of me liked being with him in the stadium that afternoon. I don't even know why.* He was cheering for the team in blue and gray, so I used their colors to reflect a stormy sky. Dad actually hung the painting in his office. I couldn't believe it. I felt ashamed at not using the colors I wanted but proud that he hung it, at the same time. When I actually go into his office (not very often), I try not to look at it. But I'm glad it's there.

"The mentorship program here is unique, but it's a special feature that, I believe, enhances the success of our graduates," Mr. Brooks continues, not having a clue what I'm thinking. That's like family, for sure. His words have the feel of a memorized speech. Does every student have to listen to this? I have an image of kids in air-conditioned offices all over the campus, listening to pompous mentors reciting in unison.

"Your roommate will be able to help you find your way around the campus, but I know questions and concerns will arise. Feel free to come to me with anything you need to discuss. My office is always open to you, and if you have a problem you should have no hesitation about calling me at home. I know you'll be an asset to our student body, Charles, and my job is to help you in any way I can."

At least it's short. I thank him, grab my pack, and get

out of the freezer. Kids are sweating in the Houston humidity outside the building, but I don't mind the weather. The sky is hazy, with a feel of rain hanging in the air, but it could be a blazing blue sky dotted with fluffy cloud shapes for all I care. I'm on the way to my studio, and grassy lawns, hedge-lined walks, and humidity are just obstacles to get past as quickly as possible.

The studio building is brick, long and narrow, so that every artist has a window on one wall—much nicer than my basement hideout at home. My parents call it a den. I know it's something of a sanctuary from eyes that slide away in discomfort (*even Steve's*), from names that hurt, from anonymous hands that tear up pictures they don't like and can't match. I'm hoping to find sanctuary in this studio, too. I crane my neck to look at the roof—seven stories up, with an intricately carved parapet at the top. I'm on the fourth floor, not too far to climb if the elevators are busy. The key turns smoothly in the outer lock, and I swing the heavy door open, dreading a rush of frigid air. But the air-conditioning here isn't so bad. If it were the same temperature as Mr. Brooks's office, the paints would harden on the palette.

Kids stumble down sleek, tiled hallways that already smell of fresh oils and turpentine, and pound up and down the polished stone stairs, trying to find their studios and get set up. Some of them look at me, wide-eyed. I'm obviously too old to be a freshman, so they wonder who I could be. I'll have to find another way into the building, where I won't have to run this gauntlet every time I come in. Maybe there's an entrance by the far stairwell.

I find my studio. There are loops for my hasp lock, above the knob. I slide the brass key into the door and swing it open, then ease inside and flip on the light. I see my crates of supplies and canvases, and I push the door shut behind me, punching the lock button. There's even a place to clasp my lock when I'm inside—the ultimate "Do Not Disturb" barrier. I slide my pack off my shoulder and pull out the heavy lock. It slips through the metal hoops and clicks solidly, locking out the world. The pack slides to the tile floor, and I lean back against the smooth wood of the door. For the first time since arriving at Whitman (*in how long really?*), I let my guard relax.

The gray light from the cloudy day washes over the plywood crates. I left some paintings locked up at home, but the ones that matter came with me. After a moment I get up and fumble with the locked clasps to open the first crate. It contains finished canvases that the audition committee most certainly did not see—canvases that might reveal too much, even to committee members who probably just want to be sure the applicant is somewhere beyond stick figures. I pull out a cityscape, a swirl of neon sunset crushed under the night, with a single bell tower glaring back at the darkness, refusing to go out. What had Mr. Brooks said about lack of discipline and perspective? He'd probably think this canvas proved his point. But it proves a different point to me.

Almost no one has seen these paintings since I showed some of them to Steve. My father might accept it if I'd stick to painting football scenes as a hobby, but pictures of phoenixes torn by lions would probably freak him out. "How are you ever going to make a living painting pictures?" he demanded before I left for Whitman. He owns a real estate business, and his idea of a good picture is a photograph that sells a house. He keeps trying to reconcile my painting with his world. "If you like to draw so much, you could be an architect," he told me once. "Or an engineer." Those are jobs he can understand.

My mother's a lawyer, and a good picture to her is one of the pretty pictures in the calendars she mails out to clients every Christmas. When I was little, she liked the pictures I made. She'd hang them on the bulletin board in her office. *Charlie's so talented...* Then she hung them on the refrigerator at home but didn't take them to her office anymore. She acted like they troubled her. *Can't you paint nice houses, and happy children playing, and pretty trees?* She wanted stick figures with big smiles on fake faces, and green lollipop trees under a blue stripe of sky. That's what other kids were painting in preschool—the kids who looked at me like I was alien because my trees actually looked like trees, and because I couldn't be bothered to waste time admiring their paint-splattered lollipops during sharing time. I was too busy trying to figure out how to do trees properly, so that the bark was textured and individual leaves rustled in the breeze. I was still trying to stripe the tree trunks and branches with black and gray and brown to give then some depth and texture, and the result wasn't as convincing as I knew I should be able to make it. What was the point, anyway, of telling some kid who'd rather be playing dodgeball that his picture was really neat, straining to sound like I meant it? I could have told him his game was great, I suppose—if I'd cared about dodgeball, beyond trying to work out how to avoid it. But what I cared about was making my painting as good, and as true, as it could possibly be.

Mother didn't care whether my trees (*or wolves*) were convincing or not. She didn't like them because they weren't like the trees other kids made. *Why don't you draw a doggy, Charlie? A dog playing with some children?* She didn't mention the pretty tree, but I knew she wanted that, too, so I made her a picture like that— a silly picture—even the stupid doggy under the lollipop tree was smiling a big fake smile. She put that one up on her bulletin board at work. *That's what people want to see, Charlie. (That's what you want to see, Mother.) You don't want to make them nervous, do you? You should make pictures like the other children do, and not make them feel sad because they can't paint the same sort of pictures.* I tried to tell her that I didn't really want to make anyone nervous—that I painted trees and wolves because I saw those pictures inside of me (*but not that I was the outcast being chased by wolf children who had banded together into a vicious pack, not because they were "sad" but because they were "ordinary" and I was different*), and I had to let them out. But she'd caught me crying from the way the other kids had hounded me. She knew the truth, even if she didn't want to think about it. *Maybe you should keep those pictures to yourself, Charlie. Simon says ... keep your art separate, keep it safe from the people who laugh at you or sneer at you, who resent your drawings.*

So I kept the real pictures to myself and gave her the fake happy pictures that I was apparently supposed to be drawing—nobody sneered at those. As I got older, though, she didn't even like that sort of picture anymore. *You're too old for that foolishness, Charlie. Boys your age don't paint all the time. You should get out and play with the other boys—take up a sport, be part of a team. And you should start thinking about what you want to do with your life. I don't understand . . .* So I showed her the real pictures I'd been painting, with the mythological symbols. I thought she'd understand if she actually saw them. After all, it wasn't wolves in stormy forests. But she only glanced at them, and then looked away. *They're very . . . nice, Charlie, but you can't spend your whole life making . . . pictures.* She sort of gestured at them, as if she couldn't even stand to look at them. At that time I still wondered why they made her so uncomfortable. Didn't she understand? Or wasn't it her? Was it me? Had I failed to get my message across? Were my pictures so bad?

If they were, the thing was to get better at them, not stop. But that wasn't what she wanted. *You're not a little boy anymore, Charlie. Painting pictures is fine for a hobby—* A hobby? Like her rosebushes, when she remembers to prune them? Or the old Mustang Dad has out in the garage, the one he's fixing up when he has an hour or two in the evening, every other week, or month, or never? A hobby? I didn't have the words then to tell her I couldn't paint just in my spare time any more than I could breathe in my spare time. But she wouldn't have listened, even if I'd had the words. *You have to make* some serious choices about your career, Charlie. What about computers? You could write game programs, with beautiful graphics. Or medicine—you could be a doctor. Or finances—you could be a stockbroker. Or, if you don't want to work at a desk, you could do something outdoors—you could be an archaeologist. Or... Anything from astrophysicist to zoologist, as long as I didn't choose painter. Paint as a hobby, Charlie, but you need to do something more with your life—something (conventional) to make us proud of you (something to justify all the effort we went through to raise you when we could have been doing other useful things like making money and being more successful like our friends. Now you owe us so we can brag about you to the other parents we know. Pay up).

I don't know how I'm going to make a living with my art, and I don't care. I could dig ditches or work in a factory—any sort of boring day job in order to pay the bills, so long as it leaves my head clear for painting.

So I cleaned out a storage room in the basement—Charlie's den for his little hobby, like Dad has the garage. I saved my allowance and birthday money for supplies, and I kept painting—in the afternoons, at least, when they were both at their jobs. Then, when they came home, I'd have dinner with them like a nice, ordinary son, and do my homework, as if I cared about the grades that were supposed to get me into college. Sometimes I'd paint again after they went to bed, or I'd get up early and paint. I'd hear the pipes when Mom took her shower and know it was time to stop. If they didn't want to see my paintings, they didn't have to see them. And neither did anybody else. *Simon says... keep your art separate...* So I made sketches in school and hid my paintings in the basement. Those sketches of the elementary school teachers who didn't like my pictures finally paid off—in middle school I started doing cartoons for the school paper. The other kids seemed to like my caricatures. So did the teachers, as long as I didn't draw them. I was pretty sure everybody liked the cartoons more than they'd like the real paintings. What a joke—caricatures in print, and all this for real.

One canvas freezes me as I crouch, flipping through the pile. Why did I bring this one? I see a portrait of a girl, beautiful, lush—not my style at all—with long silken black hair and wide, trusting blue-black eyes that pull me, drowning, into the past.

Mr. Brooks is right. I could use a class in portraiture. The canvas isn't much like the subject. When I painted it, I couldn't understand why Cindy refused to recognize herself. Now it's pretty clear. I painted love, not the girl herself. An adult would laugh at it, I guess. But it was true for me then. Looking at it now, I have to admit that Cindy was never like that. I just thought she was.

But she could have been.

It was spring of ninth grade (*after all those school art teachers, after giving up on Steve, after I should have known better*), and I had two tickets to the touring production of *Phantom of the Opera* and no date for the show. Cindy was gorgeous; I have to admit my painting doesn't lie about that. And she'd never been obnoxious to me, like the jocks and most of the other girls who went out with them. She'd even say something nice about my caricatures once in a while. Everybody was talking about the show and how hard it was to get tickets. The matinee seats were a birthday present from my mother—she wanted me to get out more and do things with other kids. I would never have expected Cindy to go out with me normally, but I thought maybe the show would be a big enough incentive to interest her. Even though I didn't really think she'd say yes, I asked her— and she did. I didn't expect to enjoy the matinee (the show was pretty glitzy), but the performance seemed to have a kind of glow about it. And so did Cindy.

She asked questions about my drawings, and she wanted to know why I didn't do more than just the cartoons in the paper and messing around in art class at school. She said she'd heard I painted some great stuff in eighth grade. I couldn't believe she'd actually been talking to the other kids about me. But Mrs. Sayers was terrific in eighth grade. I didn't show her any of my real paintings, but I did more in class than I'd done in a long time, and it was as if she could guess at the paintings she couldn't see. She was always encouraging me to try something new. In ninth grade we had a by-the-book right-and-wrong teacher who was probably afraid her students might be more creative than she was. And after what Steve had told me—well, I didn't feel like exposing much in class anymore.

Cindy and I talked all through the intermission, and then we went for pizza after the show, and I told her a little about my painting, and she seemed to listen, really listen. She didn't make fun of the idea of being an artist. Maybe she thought it was romantic. I don't know what she thought. I just looked into her blue-black eyes and talked, and she smiled up at me like what I was saying was special.

We went out a few more times and ate lunch together every day in front of all the other kids in the cafeteria. She really seemed to want them to see her with me. The kids smiled at us, secretive, unfriendly smiles, but I ignored them. I just loved being with her. Then I painted her from memory, and I knew I had to show her the portrait, and my other paintings also. Cindy would understand—unlike my mother. She wouldn't tell me it was a phase I was supposed to outgrow. Cindy wouldn't act as if there was something wrong with painting pictures that showed people there was hope beyond the wolves and the heart-crushing expectations that tried to cut you down to something petty and mediocre. I knew Cindy would *see* what I was trying to do with my paintings. And her reaction would be a taste of what I'd see on everyone's face when I had my first show. I was still young enough to think the day would come when I could show my paintings to the world.

So she came over one Thursday afternoon while my parents were at work. We sat on the couch for a while— she wanted to make out, but I couldn't get into it. No matter what I dreamed in the dark, I wanted to give her something more than just hot skin and sweaty hands in the light. I wanted to give her myself. *Stupid—I was so stupid.* I led her down to the half-finished basement, where I had my studio, and flicked on the banks of work lights. My paintings were set along the walls so she could see them. Only the best ones were out. I had others stored in cases, ones I wasn't as satisfied with but that weren't bad enough to scrape off and paint over.

Cindy saw the portrait first, and looked puzzled. Then she looked at the canvases, one by one, and said nice things, but she acted confused, almost frightened. I thought maybe she was overwhelmed—it was a lot to take in. She didn't say very much, in the end, and she didn't stay as long as I'd hoped. But I sat in my studio after she'd left, not feeling so alone there, because someone had seen my work—had really *looked,* and had really *seen.* It was the best evening I ever spent. I only went upstairs for supper, then hurried back to sit there, seeing my paintings through Cindy's eyes. I couldn't wait to see her at school the next day.

But Cindy was in a rush at her locker the next morning, and when I practically beat the bell getting out of biology to meet her for lunch, there was another guy at her locker with her—Rob Gorey, one of the basketball players. I figured she was just giving him an assignment or something, but then— She saw me, and her eyes slid away. She looked up at Rob and smiled in that special way I'd thought was just for me. My stomach clenched, and I tried to breathe but my lungs felt like balloons with the tops twisted, pressing against my rib cage. I remembered the secretive smiles. The other kids had known, all along. She'd wanted Rob from the start. She just wanted to make him jealous by going out with someone else—someone expendable. She used me. And I let her see my paintings.

Cindy laughed. She leaned against Rob and she laughed, a high splintering sound. There was a roaring in my ears, but I heard the words she spoke—something about boys who think a bunch of oily, ugly paintings is a big deal. Even though it was hard for me to hear her, I'm sure she called them ugly.

The two of them seemed spotlighted under the fluorescent lights, as if they were the only ones lit up in the crowded hallway. Cindy's black eyes flashed, and her hair wrapped around her like a shroud. Beside her, Rob stood in his black T-shirt, stiff as a poker. I stared, seeing ugly oils on canvas, and the two blacks fused, rimmed by bright lights, and my world turned black.

I skipped lunch. I skipped the afternoon. I went back to school the next day, but I skipped the rest of the year for all that. My left hand scrawled pop quizzes and then finals, but my mind was in my studio, keeping it locked, keeping my paintings safe. I promised my paintings that I had let them (*myself*) down for the last time. Mother was right: *Keep your art separate—keep those pictures to yourself.* Then I was out of middle school and away from the kids who'd known Cindy and seen her that day—the kids who'd smirked—the kids who'd known what she really thought of me. Tenth grade, starting high school, was a blank slate, and that was easier. I could play a part in the classroom (I had learned to stumble through the motions of Simon Says at last), and I could come home and hide in the basement, painting behind a locked door. I certainly never took another art class, though. I just drew cartoons for the school paper.

And I never let anyone else, not even my parents, see my paintings again, until the auditions for Whitman. If

65

I wanted to get accepted, if I wanted to meet Graeme Brandt (*if I still dreamed of someday learning how to find the courage to show my art for real*), I had no choice except to show four of them to the committee.

I stand up slowly in my new studio, my knees stiff. I slide Cindy's portrait behind another canvas—a scene of birch trees, their trunks lined up like prison bars. I want to forget I ever let her into my studio. *I can still hear her brittle laugh, shattering me.* What I do here belongs to no one but myself.

The tree-trunk-prison painting reminds me of the rustling birds in the trees. I open another case and pull out one of the canvases I'd stretched and prepared before coming here. I prop it up on my easel and lay out my palette. I sketch in the shape of looming trees in a few strokes of a yellow ocher wash, then mark off the section for the birds overhead. In the foreground, just left of center, I rough in the shape of a person. I study the proportions. Does Mr. Brooks think I need work on perspective, too? We'll see what I can take away from the class. The perspective looks right to me.

I begin mixing brown umber tones, and tree bark laced with shadows grows on the canvas. Around me, time stops. This is what I should be doing, not reliving the past but painting in the present. I flow into the paint, remembering the lowering threat of the birds half hidden in the lacework of night-dark tree branches, and pouring that feeling into the work. There's only color and texture. If I heard music right now, it would be colors exploding inside my brain. Footfalls on the stairs are muddy gray, the voices in the hall are orange flashes, seared with yellow. If I could see the students out there, they'd be moving shapes and patterns on a canvas, not threats or disappointments.

I can sense how good the painting is, how *true* it is.

I can't risk this feeling by letting anyone see the final picture. But it's not a risk, because the kid who dreamed of showing his paintings (*even as recently as last night, as recently as meeting Graeme Brandt, before seeing that he didn't have any magic answers*) is a different person now. He crippled his dreams to keep his paintings alive, fragments of color and texture barricaded within four walls and guarded by a hasp lock.

By the time I stop, the gray light outside has faded to a rainy twilight, and I've painted more than I thought. I stretch sore shoulders and look at the figure striding between the murky trees, unafraid of hidden demons, knowing they're above him, but not caring. I scrape my palette and pry open the turpentine to clean my brushes. Then I look around the studio. There's something I haven't yet unpacked.

I find it in the crate with the supplies I intend to use for art classes here. It's the only sketch I ever made of myself, before the back view on my application. This is the only one that shows my face—sort of, anyway. I drew it when I started high school. It shows me as a masked Harlequin, like one of Mother's Comedia del Arte figures, armed with my pen poised in my left hand, holding my sketch pad as a shield, standing so that I hide a draped canvas on an easel behind me. I hammer a tack into the back of the door with the body of the hasp lock and hang the sketch there. That way I can see it every time I leave the studio. It will remind me of my selves—the self that paints what could (*should*) be, and the self that caricatures what actually is—of the distinctions I don't dare forget. If only there were a way I *could* forget them.

I thought I could learn how to bring those selves together here. After reading *The Eye of the Storm,* I thought Graeme Brandt understood the dangers of being driven by other people's expectations and judgments. I thought he knew the secret of how to be himself, out where everybody could see, and not be hurt by them. I wanted him to show me how I could give up the locks and masks. But I guess I picked the wrong person to believe in (*again*). He doesn't know the secret, either.

So how did he write that book?

Excerpts from
Graeme Brandt's Journal

LETTER TO MYSELF

September 10 (Freshman Year)

Dear Graeme,

No. It might as well be Gray. As long as everybody else calls you by that nickname, you can just get used to it. Remember, you have to live up to their expectations in the little stuff—keep them happy so they'll let you have your own way in the things that matter. Always remember that.

Remember that you have to take the right courses at school. Mr. Adler told you which ones he thought you should take, and you like them because he said you would. It doesn't matter that you'd rather have taken Shakespeare than the Modern Novel; it doesn't matter that you had to write about Kazuo Ishiguro when you wanted to write about Thomas Pynchon. You learned some interesting stuff, anyway. And what really matters is that Mr. Adler is pleased that you're following his advice. He likes your work and he's excited about your writing, so do what he says.

Remember you have to hang out with the right people. This year you're rooming with Jeff Langley, and the dorm parents think he's a great guy, never a problem. Your parents like him, too, and *their* opinion is what matters. They think Whitman might be too big a step for you—they're scared you might meet weirdos who do drugs, or creative types who wear strange clothes and do embarrassing things in public.

But Jeff has short hair and calls Dad "sir," so your folks approve of him. They don't know he's probably going to flunk out his sophomore year unless you write his papers for him or his own parents can buy him passing grades. Jeff's not stupid, but he's already an alcoholic. Well...at least it's not drugs. So you don't bug him about it, and you take a drink when he offers, even if you sip it very slowly. Jeff likes you to look up to him as someone who knows his way around, who can show you the ropes at Whitman. And your parents like to think he's keeping you out of trouble. Let them think that, if it makes them happy—they're going to think it anyway.

Remember that, Gray: People think what they want to. You'll please them all the more by making whatever they think seem real for them. It's so easy. It takes so little effort to please people. You don't have to lie to any of them, either. Just show them whatever part of yourself you know they'll like.

Remember that you have to date the right girls. Your parents like to hear about your dates because they don't want you to work all the time, they want you to have some fun. Your friends expect you to date because they do, and seeing other people doing the same thing makes us all feel we're doing the right thing, doesn't it?

When you date, take the girls where they want to go: Please them. It's so easy—the other guys take their dates to hard-core action movies and football games and things that *they* like. You can make the girls happy by taking them to romantic movies, or to plays or concerts. It doesn't make any difference to you, anyway. It's all the same.

And it's easy, after all, to find friends you really do like to be with. Jeff introduced you to Ben Carter, so your parents approve of him. And the teachers see Ben as one of their promising seniors: He's already had a one-act considered by the Humana Festival—it's not Broadway, but it's national theater, not just school. So Mr. Adler thinks it's great that Ben's taken you under his wing. Well, Ben opened up a whole new world for you. Ben's gay, and he showed you things you only dreamed of—things you thought no one else imagined except you. Girls are easy enough to date, but if they get serious it gets harder and harder to please them. Guys are so much easier to keep happy, and perhaps you like them better. Ben does, and you like Ben.

Boys—girls—just satisfy whoever you're with, Gray. It's easy to please all of them, after all. Spend your time with Ben and his friends, and take out girls to please your parents and your other friends. Everybody knows they're just living up to everybody else's expectations, and everybody pleases themselves by believing whatever they like to believe about themselves and about everyone else, and ignoring things that might upset them, right?

You've found the real secret, Gray. This is what people are, here and now. This is what they all do, and you're going to write about these people. In that class on the modern novel, Mrs. Wilson said that a novelist's task is to define people within the novelist's time. Well, this is your time, and this is what people are like, so this is what you'll write.

Ben likes what you write. Your mother likes the fact that you write, without caring exactly what it *is* you're writing. Mr. Adler loves your style and your insight. Your father thinks it's a strange career, but he's proud of your good grades. Everyone's pleased with you—your friends, the teachers, everyone you meet—you're living up to their expectations, and they're all pleased to see what they want.

It's so easy, Gray.

August 31 (Senior Year)

[Note to myself now—if it was all so easy then, what's changed now? If I knew the answers, were the answers wrong? Or are there simply more answers because the questions have gotten harder? Sometimes I think I can't find anything to fill the empty hole because there's nothing to find, but that doesn't make the emptiness hurt less. There has to be a better answer, somewhere. When I write, I want to feel like Karl feels when he sculpts. I want someone to look at me and see me lost in my creation. I want to create something worth getting lost in.]

September 21 (Freshman Year)

It's all coming into place. Now that I know what to write, the words are spilling out onto the page. It's churning inside me like a storm, and that's what I'm going to call it: *The Eye of the Storm.* Jeff thinks it's weird I'm in my studio writing so much, but I know he's actually scared about his own classes rather than worried about me, so I've been helping him with an English paper when I'm in our room. And Ben really understands—he knows I'm writing.

Was there ever such a high? Everything seems brighter around me, the colors of the changing leaves, the tangy autumn scent on the breeze, the damp grass underfoot. And everywhere I go, there's my main character, Alan Travis, turning to talk to me, or talking through me to one of the other characters in the book. He's growing, and he's going to make it because he knows the secret.

Sometimes I wonder what it would be like to have somebody actually read this book. This isn't like the short stories I've written, or the papers I write for class. There's so much of me in Alan's story that I don't really know what an outside reader would make of it. I know what I want them to make of it—I want them to nod and see themselves in it, and I want them to think about themselves differently than they had before. A writer shows his reader things he hadn't known before, not just so the reader can say, "Sure, that's how it is," but so the reader can think about those things from a new perspective. That's what I'm showing them: a new perspective on playing the game.

February 16 (Freshman Year)

When Mr. Adler said he wanted to speak to me first thing this morning, he sounded so serious I wondered if Jeff's English teacher could have told him I'd written Jeff's paper on Tom Stoppard's plays. But it was about *The Eye of the Storm.* He'd already finished reading it, and he was blown away (couldn't resist!). Totally. He wants to give it to this agent he knows, and he thinks it's going to be *published*! I'm stunned. I mean—that's what I wanted. But still—it's a long way from dreaming something to seeing it really happen.

But Mr. Adler is thrilled, because the teachers all give each other credit when one of them mentors a student who succeeds. And they usually have to wait until a kid's a senior, or at least a junior, to start bragging. So he's going to get credit for mentoring me and maybe getting me published as a freshman! Fine with me. And he likes me all the more for thanking him and letting him think I believe he had something important to do with it. Maybe he did.

At lunchtime I called my mom to tell her the good news, and she was satisfied—not shrieking and everything, just satisfied, like it was the very least of what she's been expecting all along. "I knew everything I sacrificed for you was worth it," she told me, and her voice sounded more peaceful than triumphant. But that's fine with me. This is just going to be the start.

Now I've got this idea for an essay on writing that I want to submit to the student journal, *Ventures*. I think they'll take it. Maybe the next step would be to get on staff there. I'm really doing it!

Spring Break, April 17 (Freshman Year)

This is better than all the chocolate rabbits and foil-wrapped marshmallow eggs piled high in a fantasy Easter basket! Mr. Adler called me at home. The agent he got placed *The Eye of the Storm*! No joke! Fifteen (just), and I'm going to have a major publishing house publish my novel! My parents are delighted. This time Mom did start shrieking. I'm going to dedicate the book to Mom and Dad—they should really like that.

Everybody wants to celebrate. My parents were planning this Easter picnic—now they're turning it into a party announcing the book, and Mr. Adler is planning a big party for the writing arts department as soon as we all get back to Whitman. I called Ben, and we're planning our own celebration of the contract. Suddenly I'm a celebrity, and the book isn't even out yet! But Mr. Adler said something about fast-tracking publication so it'll come out early next spring, right after everybody gets back to school from Christmas break.

THE NEW YORK TIMES   FEBRUARY 6

by Alvin Pierce

The Eye of the Storm
by Graeme Brandt. 223 pages.

In these confusing times it is astounding to discover an author who dares to offer explanations for modern Americans, and their mental peccadilloes, without embarrassment or apologies. It is more astounding still when the author is a boy. Newcomer Graeme Brandt is just that: fifteen, and he has presented young readers with an imperfect but nevertheless impressive first novel.

It is as if a surgeon took his scalpel and carved out the very core of our youth, then exposed with painful clarity exactly what keeps today's kids going. There is no gentleness in Brandt's language or theme; everything is diamond sharp and uncompromising in the terrifying voice of matter-of-fact high school student Alan Travis.

The Eye of the Storm is a character study that traces Alan's rise from street life in San Francisco with his homeless father and younger brother to a private high school in Los Angeles. Brandt sees America as an environment tailored to yes-men, and has Alan drag his family to the top by striving to please everyone around him and by teaching his out-of-luck father and his admiring brother to do the same. It's a precarious road to success, threatening to veer off into disaster at any turn.

As the Travis family climbs, we don't know whether to cheer Alan on or to deplore his tactics, but he so resembles that part of ourselves that we hate to acknowledge that we cannot ignore him. Brandt flings Travis at us with an analytical accuracy that will shake the reader and keep him in knots long after he turns the final page.

Although this novel is marred by youthful overexuberance, Graeme Brandt is more than a precocious teenager. He is well on his way to shouldering the responsibility of the novelist's art to define us for ourselves. Few authors have effectively confronted this monumental task since William Faulkner captured the Southern mind so clearly—and fewer still have ever done it deliberately for young people.

That's not to say that adults won't be mesmerized by this novel. Read it to discuss with your teenagers, because they'll be talking about Alan Travis—and about Graeme Brandt. Whether your reaction is fury or resentment at helpless recognition, remember that this is the America you live in. Watch Brandt to see what he writes next; perhaps he can tell us where we're going.

Mr. Adler said that the *Times* doesn't review many books for kids and teens, so it's a big deal that they gave the book such a great review. I guess it's great, even though Mr. Pierce doesn't seem to like what I had to say much—he likes the book more than Tyler Murdoch did here at Whitman, though! The review in *Ventures* was pretty bad—a prophet in his own land, I guess. But the book got good reviews in *Publishers Weekly* and *School Library Journal,* and a bunch of other magazines I've never heard of. And it's in the book fair, which means they'll take it right into the schools so kids can buy it easier.

The agent has taken a collection of my short stories to see if he can sell it to the same publisher, or maybe to a different one. And *Ventures* did take the essay. It's like I can't put a wrong word on paper, even if I try.

My parents are thrilled about the book's success, though my dad had to warn me it might not last. I don't know about that. Even though I'm not working on a new novel yet, I'm full of ideas for stories, and maybe something will grow to book size. I'm not sure I knew this was going to be a book when I started it, though I was hoping, certainly.

But right now I'm just enjoying the fuss. Even seniors at Whitman recognize me and talk to me around the campus! Not that most of them have read the book, of course. But some of them have, and others have read the reviews, and nearly everyone has heard about it. They all have their own impressions of me—and all the impressions are different. I think that's interesting.

4

"It's for you," Adrian calls out, waving the phone receiver in my direction. "Or are you asleep there?"

Lying on my bed and staring at the ceiling is far from sleep. I can see patterns in the textured plaster; I can make colors on the white backdrop. It's better than thinking.

I roll off the bed and take the phone.

"Charles?" It's my father.

"Charlie? Are you all right?" And my mother.

"Hi. I'm fine. All settled in."

My mother asks, "You haven't forgotten your promise, have you?"

I had to work at getting them to let me come to Whitman, even with the scholarship. My mother was horrified that I was still so obsessed with painting. I finally made a deal with them—I'd get decent grades in the academic courses I took, and I'd take all the tests, and next year I'd fill out applications for colleges, and once I graduated I'd go to college and study for a sensible profession. Mother said they'd let me come here as long as I understood it was sort of a last fling before I put aside my "childhood love of painting" and settled down to their idea of a "sensible career."

"I haven't forgotten," I tell her.

"Are they teaching you anything there?" my father asks.

Not about perspective in still lifes or landscapes. But I don't tell him that. "Sure," I say instead. "I'm reading *Lord Jim* in English, and I'm taking Introductory Programming, like you suggested."

"That's good," he says eagerly. "There are some good jobs in programming—with lots of emphasis on graphics these days. Are they teaching you how to write programs for video games?"

My sudden smile—at his struggle to reconcile my art with something practical like computers—takes me by surprise. I ought to tell him I wouldn't be caught dead writing computer programs for a living any more than I'd be caught dead sitting in an office selling real estate or being a lawyer, but I can't shape the words. I'm too pleased to hear his voice. "Maybe. It's a two-semester course, so we could get into that in the spring. Or next year."

"Did your art things get there safely?" Mother asks.

Things. "Yeah. The studio's all set up now."

"Now don't lock yourself in that studio and forget about your other courses," she warns. *It's time you got this out of your system once and for all, Charlie.*

"I won't." I change the subject. "Hey, the editor of the art and literary journal here asked me to do some sketches she can publish."

"Congratulations!" Dad says, a little too heartily.

Mother says, "Send us copies."

Right. What's she planning to do—stick them up on the refrigerator like the lollipop trees and stick figures with fake smiles? Show them to the DA next time he visits her office about a case? "Sure."

"And talk to your counselor," she continues, "or, what is he called? Your mentor? About courses you need to take so you're ready for those college applications next year. And ask about financial aid applications, too."

"That's a year away," my father tells her. "He's taking good courses. He'll get good grades before it's time to send in applications."

"I just want him to remember his grades are important," she says sharply. "If it weren't for the fact that he got a scholarship to Whitman, we couldn't afford to send him there." Her tone is resentful.

"Well, I'm sorry the economy was down and it was a tough year for moving real estate," Dad snaps. "We've got savings set aside for his college."

"It's just that college tuition is so expensive," my mother frets. "Those savings may not be enough."

I've heard all this before. Did they only call to argue with each other across the extensions? "I'm doing fine in classes," I interrupt. "There won't be any trouble with the college applications." And there won't. I may not even go to college, despite what I promised them. I would have said anything to get them to let me come here so I could meet Graeme Brandt. I still can't quite believe he's not what I'd imagined.

"You're sure, now?" Mother says doubtfully. Maybe

80

she suspects I'm willing to lie for my paintings, if I have to. "Your transcripts are important, Charlie. Remember our agreement—if you don't make good enough grades this semester, you'll have to come back—"

"He knows," Dad tells her. "Don't worry, Charles. I'm sure you're studying. We just wanted to say hi and make sure you're off to a good start."

"I am—everything's going to be fine," I assure (*lie to*) him. "And I'm glad you called." *Strangely, not a lie.*

"Let us know if you need anything," Dad adds.

"I will. Thanks."

Adrian sighs as I hang up the phone. "How nice. How can politicians wonder where family values have gone? Even just hearing one side of the conversation, I think it's clear we have a real American family here: hardworking, respectable parents calling their artistic son to make sure he's all right."

I suspect he's itching to ask me about my relationship with my parents so he can tell me about his. All I answer is, "Yeah." But I can't help studying him as he sits at his desk, the bright light creating a silhouette as he faces into the room. Only the outer edges of his hair have any color—a rusty halo framing his shadowed face. I'd like to paint that image.

"You know," he says, "some guys actually get homesick here. Boarding school—first time away from home and all? That's one of the reasons for putting new kids in with survivors. We provide sympathy and comfort." I can hear a smile in his voice, like he's joking, only I can hear he's not, too.

When I don't answer, he adds, lightly, "So if you feel

homesick, just let me know." His tone sharpens. "Or do calls from home ease the ache within?"

Not the real ache. But I don't want to talk about me. "Don't your parents ever call?"

The halo of hair shudders as he shakes his head. "They've gotten me out of the way so I'm not an embarrassment," he says flippantly. "Tuition here is a small price to pay to forget about me. They'll fork over money for college after I graduate, as long as I promise never to come back home."

Before I can stop myself I ask, "They're not music lovers?"

Adrian laughs, and it's not a pleasant sound. "They like music all right. It's *me* they can't stand."

I guess they don't like his being gay. Well, he could hide it if he wanted to, the way I hide my paintings. Who's really homesick here? I think it's Adrian, for what he wishes he had. More than me, anyway. "Well, if you miss having attentive parents, feel free to talk to mine anytime."

"I can borrow them? How sweet." I can tell from his tone that he's smiling now, even though the backlighting still hides his face.

I reach for my pack, and he asks, "Off to your studio?" He drawls the words as though they don't matter, but I hear a trace of disappointment.

"Yeah. A still-life project due." I watch him pick up his headphones. "How come you're never in your studio?" I ask suddenly. "Aren't you supposed to be composing music, not just listening to it?"

He laughs, fluttering his fingers at me limply. "You're in your studio such long hours, dear, you have no idea how much I've written since school started!"

I almost wince at the wave and the casual "dear," including me as if I were like him, and I guess he can see something (*disgust*) on my face. He turns away, and with his face no longer silhouetted by the light I see his smile fade. Well, it's his own fault, for acting like that. "Why do you do that?" I blurt out. "Can't you at least try to sound—I don't know—normal?"

For a moment Adrian just sits there, his eyes fixed on his limp-wristed hand gently dangling the headphones. Then he slowly rises, his fingers tightening into a fist around the band connecting the earpieces. Instead of easing into his customary slouch, he draws himself straighter, until he's taller than I suspected. He pushes his shoulders back, clenches his other fist and thrusts out his jaw. He glares at me and drops his voice nearly an octave, demanding in a brusque, aggressive tone, "Is this what you'd prefer? Do you think I'd pass like this at some football tailgate party?" And the scary thing is— yes, I think he would.

Then his face dissolves into a wry smile, his posture relaxes, and his voice slides up to its regular pitch. "Though why I'd want to be caught dead at some jock tailgate party is beyond me."

He drops the headphones on his desk, and suddenly his hazel eyes are serious. "Sounding like that—acting like that—that's playing games, and I won't do it. This—" Adrian spreads his hands helplessly—proudly.

"This is me. No games. Just me. And I won't pretend to be anyone else. Not for anybody."

I bow my head, embarrassed (*by what I said, or by how he answered?*), and turn away. I half expect him to call me back, but he's silent as I head out of the room, shutting the door behind me (*shutting him firmly out of my mind*), then follow the tree-lined walk into the main campus, trying to think about the new painting I'm working on.

The birds canvas is done, and I've discovered you can go up to the roof of the studio building. Most days it's too hot, but after dark it's almost like sitting in the stars, high above the trees, above the birds. There aren't even as many mosquitoes up there. I've started a painting of stars—a clear, shimmering night sky, with just the hint of buildings straining up at the edges of the image, like teeth ready to slice the sky to shreds. I thought about turning it in to my Landscape class, but why risk it? Instead, I'm doing a field. With cows. And a barn. Even a silo. *Sigh.* At least the cows aren't smiling.

Still Life is the worst, though. The teacher—a short, balding man with bushy eyebrows and a chip on his shoulder the size of a mural—reminds me of Mr. Birkin from third grade.

"And what is that, Mr. Weston?" He acts like it's a major sign of respect to call us by our last names while he's ripping into us.

"It's a pile of books, Mr. Wallace."

"It is not the pile of books on that table." He shakes a bony finger at the still life setting.

I study the table. "You see, the Dickens was crying

out for Thackeray instead of that paperback Melville. And the book that's propped open really needed an illustration on the left-hand page to balance the color of the spines on the books behind it. I just added in what was missing." I'm not in third grade anymore.

Someone smothers a giggle behind me. Mr. Wallace stares at my canvas. "You just added in what *you* thought was missing?"

More giggles, and a loud chuckle.

I look at my painting, at the balance I created from his chaos. "Yes sir."

He raps a brush hard on the top stretcher bar of my canvas. "That is not the purpose of this class, Mr. Weston! The purpose is to paint what you see."

That is *what I see, you moron. The purpose of art is to interpret, to express, not just to make a cheap photocopy.* I stare at him, and he suddenly backs away from me a step. "We are starting fruit tomorrow," he tells me. "I will give you another chance." His voice is shaking—with anger? with fear? with what?

Sure enough, we start fruit. I dutifully rough in a blue-and-white uneven potter's bowl, and a tasty (if not tasteful) pile of apples and oranges and pears and grapes. There's a bruise on one of the pears, a nice study in hazels. I wonder if he'll replace the pear before it discolors completely, but each night he carefully puts the bowl into the refrigerator, and each afternoon, takes it out for our class.

I told Adrian I had to work on that still life, but I don't. It's going disgustingly well. I switch on autodraw and the colors ooze around on the canvas. Maybe I could write a computer program that does that for you, takes a photograph of something and scans it in, then lets you paint it like a fill-in-the-numbers chart—a salvation program for artists who are trapped by creation-destroying teachers.

Actually, I'm not even going to my studio. I have an appointment to see Rachel Holland. I don't know why I didn't just tell Adrian that. I push open one of the heavy bronze doors at the student center and remember him opening it for me the night I met Graeme Brandt. *Adrian says . . . show time!* Another performance.

The elevator has doors you have to pull open—an old-fashioned cage that stinks of machine oil as it creaks and shudders and strains its way up to the third floor. You'd think Whitman could afford a newer model. Maybe they think it adds to the charm. Maybe I should take the stairs down. It's all too easy to imagine this thing shuddering to a halt, trapped between floors. Actually, with the sketch pad in my pack that wouldn't be so bad. A few hours out of time, with nobody telling me what to draw. But it's even easier to see the ancient cables snapping at last, twanging like shots in the elevator shaft as the metal cage crashes toward the basement. I'm not ready for that, at least not yet.

Glass windows line the hallway to make the place look bigger—maybe to let the kids see out of their cages. The *Ventures* office is at the end of the hall, silent outside the glass, a chaos of activity inside.

"You're new around here," a girl says, looking up at me briefly from a computer screen. "Whatcha need?"

"Where's Rachel?"

The girl looks at me more carefully. "She's really busy, y'know? We're putting together the first issue, and it's always a panic."

So? "She told me to come by."

"Yeah? What's your name?"

"Charles Weston. If you just point in the right direction—"

"Come on," she says, punching a button on her keyboard and jumping up—the tight jeans and stretched T-shirt type. She glances at me over her shoulder to make sure I've noticed. "I'm Buffy," she tells me.

Of course she is...

I follow her, threading my way between computer desks and tables with unruly stacks of papers and file cabinets with drawers half open. She knocks on a closed door, half hidden between two tall file cabinets, then pushes it open.

"Rachel? There's a Charles Weston here asking for you?"

"Good. How's the layout coming?"

Buffy shrugs one shoulder. "I've got all the headlines and subs set, y'know? I'm playing with caption highlights now."

"I'll take a look when I'm done with Charles."

Buffy eases out of the doorway and grins at me. "Go on in."

I shut the door behind me. Like magic, an oasis of calm in a disaster area. "How do you get anything done in this place?" I ask.

Rachel smiles from behind a desk lined with in- and out-boxes neatly stacked with papers and file folders. "I have a door and I keep it closed."

I smile back, knowing that solution all too well, and slide into a chair. File cabinets and shelves line the walls in here as well, except for a window that lets in a square of blue sky and a wedge of sunlight. It makes me think of a dormer window, the way it's framed between the file cabinets. Across the tops of the cabinets, and at the ends of the rows of books on the shelves, there are wooden shapes—puzzles, I realize. The kind where you have to pull a brass ring over a ball or a disk that's bigger than the ring. And a Labyrinth game with a steel ball bearing you have to maneuver around a maze without it falling into holes. "You like puzzles?" I ask.

She reaches for one and idly slides the ball and trapped ring back and forth on the cord that runs into the wooden base. "I like seeing into things and working out how they fit." She looks up at me. "That's why I like your sketches. You see into people, how the pieces of them fit together, and then you draw what you see so that other people can understand them."

I shrug uncomfortably, thinking of the way I've drawn so many teachers over the years. It's true—I knew just what to draw to hurt them the way they'd hurt me. I still hate them, and the kids who attacked more bluntly, but I wish I could find a way to deal with them other than stooping to their level and hurting them back. What I draw is true, even if it hurts, but hurting people doesn't make them change.

I don't like the way my thoughts are headed—and I

don't like the way Rachel is sitting back, observing me through her clear brown eyes (*not blue-black like Cindy's eyes, not admiring me the way Cindy's eyes seemed to do*). I don't want her to think she understands me (*to think she likes me*) from seeing me sketch. Next thing, she'll want to be friends, and then she'll want to see my paintings, and then her eyes will slide away, the way Mrs. Geller's did, the way Steve's did (*or she'll laugh, like Cindy*).

Abruptly I break contact, the way I did when I walked away from Adrian earlier, except now I feel a strange tightness in my chest, as if I can't breathe. There's not enough air in her small office. My eyes drop down to my sketch of Tyler dueling with the mirror, neatly centered on her blotter. What would Mr. Wallace say about that example of "drawing what I see"? That steadies me. "Okay. So who did you have in mind for this article on the seniors?"

She sets the puzzle aside, pulls out a file folder, and opens it. "We're planning to feature Marc Worley—he's a director from the drama department. And Sara Hoffman, a poet. I'd like to include Kikuei Isomura, a pianist, but I'm not sure there's enough substance there. Why don't you talk to him and tell me what you think?"

She rattles off more names I don't recognize, and I pull out my sketch pad and jot them down on a blank page. My handwriting is spiky at first, then it settles down.

"And Graeme Brandt, of course." *Of course.* "Do you have a feel for him yet?"

I snap shut the sketch pad. "Not yet," I tell her.

She nods. "He's difficult," she offers. "I've published several of his essays, but I don't feel I know him."

I change the subject. "Why editing? Why don't you write, yourself?"

She smiles. "I do! More than just the editorial in every issue—I'm working on a novel. But there's something about editing...I read a manuscript and I can see the potential in it, even if the author hasn't done her idea justice. I see what she wants to say, and I shape the piece to say it more clearly."

But what if you see something different than the author intended? At least she can't do that with artwork, I reassure myself.

"Of course," she adds, "that's only with writing. I can't do much shaping with a caricature—though if I think you need to clarify something I'll point it out and ask you to redo it."

As if there's anything she could see that I'd need to clarify! "Strange job," I mutter.

"I suppose so," she says, undisturbed by my lack of enthusiasm. "But I think it's exciting to look inside something and find its potential and let it out." She turns back to her file folder. "I'd like to run this piece before Thanksgiving." She adds to her neat hieroglyphic notes. "Will you be able to see them all and work up the sketches by then?"

"Unless I flunk out," I quip, but Rachel doesn't laugh. She studies me as though I'm one of her puzzles, or a manuscript with hidden potential that requires considerable editing. I slide the sketch pad back into my pack. "If I run into trouble with any of them, I'll let you know."

"Good. How're classes?"

Her calm, interested tone unbalances me, and I answer before thinking. "Landscape is a bore and Still Life is torture—" Then I interrupt myself, realizing she's listening too closely. She wanted me to expose myself, the way she wants to expose the seniors in this article. Well, forget it. "But I'll survive. I may even learn something in spite of myself."

"Don't let Wallace ruin you," she tells me, her fingers playing idly with the ring on the puzzle. "Who's your mentor?"

"Mr. Brooks."

"Talk to him if Still Life gets too bad."

What does she know? It was Brooks who put me there. "Anyone can paint a bowl of fruit on autodraw." I almost tell her about my idea for a computer program oozing colors onto a scanned photo, but I stop myself. This isn't a friend, despite her clear brown eyes that seem to see too much and still smile. This is an editor— an editor who digs inside things (*manuscripts, paintings, people*) to put the pieces together more efficiently. "Thanks for the advice, though."

Rachel looks at me thoughtfully, then deftly slips the wooden puzzle piece attached to one side of the cord through a slot in the base. She eases the brass ring over the doubled cord, then slides the ring through the slot, and up and over the base to freedom. She smiles and stands, replacing the solved puzzle on its shelf and setting the brass ring beside it. "I have to check Buffy's layout."

As I stand aside to let her lead the way out of her office, I see the tops of the file cabinets. Not all of the decorations are puzzles. She also has a collection of kaleidoscopes perched on wooden stands. Maybe Rachel's fascination with the puzzles and kaleidoscopes is more than just seeing inside something (*somebody?*) to see how it works. Maybe she takes things apart to find the potential hidden in the fragments. But how can she be so sure her reassembled pieces are an improvement?

5

"So you *have* been working!" I drop my backpack on my bed and stare at the program he's handed me. The second performance is String Quartet in G Minor by Adrian Lawson.

"I worked on it last summer, actually," he admits, blushing. "I've just been polishing it up this semester."

"And rehearsing it," I point out. I look up, delighted for him and amazed at the risk he's taking by letting everyone listen to his music. Isn't he afraid that people will hear what he can do and resent him for it? Or does he expect people to resent him anyway, because he's gay and doesn't hide it? Or does he simply think it's good enough for the teachers, but not exceptional enough to disturb anyone? Somehow, none of these feels like the real explanation. "I can't wait to hear it."

"You really want to come?" Adrian sounds surprised. "It's not all that great," he warns, flapping his hands awkwardly as if he doesn't know where to put them. "Well, it is kind of neat—with lots of string plucking instead of bowing—but it's pretty derivative, too..."

Maybe he really doesn't think it's very good. I won't know until I hear it, so I just joke, "Quit criticizing yourself before Tyler does it for you." Then I add, not certain why, "It's got to be good, or they wouldn't be performing it, right?"

"Well..." He hunches one shoulder and looks unconvinced.

"I really want to come," I assure him.

"We're having kind of a party after," he says slowly, "to celebrate. I don't suppose you'd want to go to that..." He lets the words trail off.

I almost groan. Trapped. But I am curious about his music. "Yeah, sure. As your roommate, not your date," I add quickly.

He smiles. "Of course."

≡

Adrian was wrong—his music is terrific. And I like the odd voice of the plucked strings—like a harp, instead of the whining bows that usually give me a headache in string music. Adrian manages to make the strings sing and purr and hum. I could paint shafts of silver light in a blue-gray wash that would shimmer like those strings.

I glance behind me in the school concert hall. Adrian stands at the back of the rows of seats, a stiff shadow dimly illuminated by the glow of the exit lights. He holds his arms folded tightly across his chest, one fist pressed against his mouth as if he's gnawing his knuckles. Is that what it's like to have a crowd of people studying your work? It was bad enough with one. Why does he do it?

94

Turning back to the four musicians on the stage, I see Tyler slumped in an aisle seat a few rows in front of me, probably imagining himself a critic for the *New York Times,* ready to jump from his seat at the curtain and race to his office to dash off his latest poison-pen review. He'll probably burn Adrian to a crisp to get even for my sketch. I ignore the pang of regret and let the music wash over me.

After the final movement, I grab my pack and slip out of my seat during the applause. I corner Adrian in the lobby as he's heading out to circle around to the stage entrance. "It was great," I tell him honestly.

The awkward tension has drained out of him, and he looks radiant, almost luminous, like that dazzling music. *Is that why you risk it? To become part of that radiance?* "Go—" I give him a slight push toward the stage. "Enjoy. I'll be back for the party."

I let myself into the dark, away from the lighted building, away from the people. The party will be here, in the concert-hall lobby, but I want some time alone first. I walk through the night, listening to the strains of music in my memory. A fresh wind blows into my face, not hot for once. We'll have rain later on, the drops echoing the sound of the plucked strings. The wind in the leaves hums like the violins singing; the clouds scud across a quarter moon like the mellow drone of the cello. I lean into the wind, into the sounds, and the world feels new-made and full of promise.

I see a single tree illuminated by a street lamp. It stands out starkly against the swirling grays of the sky, bent sideways by years of wind. The trunk and branches have allowed the wind to cripple them rather than break under its onslaught. I stare, transfixed by the sharp, clear image of the tree against the sky, painting it in my mind as color and texture on a waiting canvas.

Why couldn't I have someone to share this moment with? Someone who understands tormented trees fighting ceaseless winds in a canvas world? There *has* to be someone, somewhere, to whom I could describe this tree and the things it makes me feel—even someone who could see the tree and know how I feel without my saying a word. Someone who could look at the painting I'll make of this twisted trunk and gnarled branches— hunched even on a still day against the winds that have tried to beat it down in the past and will come back, again and again—and understand the feelings mixed with the oils. Other people have friends who share their dreams.... For a slow moment, the longing is piercingly sweet.

Then I turn away from the crippled tree. Other people open themselves up, the way Adrian opened himself tonight by having his music played. They've found a place to belong, a way to be accepted for themselves. Why is it so much easier for them than it is for me? Why am I the one who doesn't belong anywhere—isn't accepted anywhere? I can't risk opening myself up, not the way Graeme risked opening himself in his book. Or did he? Adrian's self was in his music tonight, just as my self is in my painting. I thought Graeme's self was in his book, but the pieces don't fit together. Is that really why Rachel wants me to sketch him? Because she wants someone to rearrange the pieces so they fit?

I head back toward the concert hall, drawn by the light of the party. The music crowd seems delighted with Adrian's quartet and excited about the opening concerto for oboe and violin composed by a senior, Kayla Swenson. She's not one of the ones Rachel suggested I sketch. I wonder why. Adrian is still glowing, but I don't go over to him. He reads my feelings too well—no point in letting my lonely ache sour his evening's high.

"So—who're you skewering tonight?"

The sharp voice cuts into my retreat and I look up, edgy. Tyler is glaring at me. "Enjoy the music?" I ask him.

He snorts. "That cheap copy of Debussy and Ravel?"

For a second I'm lost. Then I remember Adrian telling me apologetically that the quartet was pretty derivative, and I think of the Ravel CDs scattered around the room. Plenty of Stravinsky and Rachmaninoff, but I can't recall seeing Debussy. Not that I've listened to any of them. But I'll bet Tyler hasn't, either, and I decide to bluff. "I'm surprised you could recognize the influence of Ravel, Tyler. I thought your specialty was words. Not Debussy, though. He's not as high on Adrian's list. I hope you didn't put that in your review."

For an instant, panic flares in Tyler's eyes. Then he counters, "Ravel clearly based his quartet on Debussy's!"

I knew I was right to sketch him as a fencer. I offer a mock gasp. "What—Ravel a plagiarist? And Adrian, too?"

Somebody snickers and Tyler's expression darkens. "Someday we'll see if you play with colors as well as you play with words." He practically spits at me. "If you ever dare to show your paintings and let anyone critique them, that is."

I feel like I'm the one who just got skewered. It was a stupid idea to come, to let myself in for this.

"Anyone but you, dear. You wouldn't have a clue." Adrian's voice is light and amused as he suddenly appears beside me. "Anyway, I thought dares were for grade school. Aren't you a little old for that game? Now run along and stir up some other mischief. Try telling Kayla that she copied Bach and see how she likes it."

Without waiting for a response, Adrian heads to the concession stand and I follow. I shy away from the sweet caffeine and get a ginger ale. As we stand there together, I watch the carbonation fizz in the plastic glass.

"I'm afraid you've made an enemy," Adrian comments, not blaming me because Tyler's going to roast his music for my sake.

I shrug and smile faintly. "Yeah. I wonder how Tyler got in here. What did he do to audition? Drag Sondheim's latest over the coals to demonstrate his reviewing abilities?"

Adrian glances over his shoulder. "Actually," he says thoughtfully, "Tyler's a very good writer. He had a couple of essays in *Ventures* before he started writing reviews, and I believe he's working on a play. But I've also heard he's a terrible perfectionist—he agonizes over every syllable. I think he finds it easier to criticize other people's work because he's dissatisfied with his own."

I can't believe Adrian's actually excusing him. "Well, thanks for the rescue."

He turns back to me and his face lights up. I almost regret my smile. But I can't help liking Adrian for his music, and maybe even just for himself. Anyway, he deserves something for stepping in and distracting Tyler from my painting. I don't like owing anybody, but I don't know how to pay him back without letting him expect too much. It's hard to like someone and hold them at arm's length, knowing their eyes will slide away uncomfortably and they won't like you if they get too close. Then I almost snap my fingers.

"What's that for?"

How did he see the thought hit me? I ignore the question and grin, and my tone matches the lightness in his, although I can hear that his is forced. "I was just thinking I hadn't done any sketching tonight—seems the perfect way to say thanks."

"Oh, no," he says quickly. "You don't owe me anything."

And I suppose I don't. But I suddenly think of the crippled tree and wonder—if Adrian can write that music, would he understand that tree? "Wait till you see the sketch," I tell him, leaning in toward him slightly so I can keep my voice low.

Across the room, I see Rachel talking to the cellist, smiling at the girl. Forgetting about Adrian, I smile, too, a wave of excited pleasure surging up inside of me. I think of the way Rachel looks inside people, trying to see how the pieces fit together. Would *she* understand the bent tree? Are there actually people here at Whitman that I might be able to share it with? She looks up and sees me. She's wearing a dress tonight, a soft green that ripples in the light like leaves in the sun (*like leaves dappled with the shadows of fluttering birds*). Her even brown gaze smiles into mine, and the party fades around us as I catch my breath.

Then Adrian pulls back slightly, and I see the scene in sharp focus—tense kids, already trapped in roles they've chosen for reasons they can't even understand. And, disembodied, I see myself, posing as the deliberately casual, almost—but not quite—too intimate friend of my gay roommate, while Adrian plays the companion role of flinching at our being caught together.

I recoil from the insight. Still staring at Rachel's face, I see the reflection of my widening eyes in hers. Just before I can shove Adrian away, my mind grabs control and forces the scene back into perspective. My mentor would be pleased to see my growing grasp of perspective. It's just a party. Adrian's just my roommate. *My friend?* And Rachel is just my editor, nothing more. Not a seer whose cool eyes look too deep. Not someone I could care about. Across the room, Rachel turns back to the cellist.

As she does, I touch Adrian's arm lightly. "Wait till you see it," I repeat, and watch his uncertainty fade and be replaced with something like relief.

Then I straighten and turn away. Just a party. Just a lot of kids like me, trying to figure out how to make their own art or find their own voice. *Or how to belong.* Only, they're not just like me. . . . Still, it's only a party.

I go into the concert hall itself. A few students hang around in the aisles, on the stage even, talking to each other, maybe even listening to what the others say. But it's less crowded in here. I walk down an empty row to a seat against the right-hand wall, under a sconce light. I pull out my sketch pad and sit holding it, going over the sketch in my mind.

"Hiding out?" There is no accusation in Rachel's voice, and none in her cool eyes as I look up. Her dress rustles softly as she makes her way across the row of seats in front of me and stands there, her back to the stage.

"Maybe."

"Sketching?"

I'm glad I haven't started yet. "Not for *Ventures*," I tell her. "This is just a gift. A thank-you."

She doesn't pursue it. Instead, she cocks her head to one side, and the light slides across her shining cap of hair. I imagine painting the strands, using the texture from a coarse brush to give each delicate hair life. She asks, "Are you with Adrian Lawson tonight, or someone else?"

I glance down at the sketch pad. Why should she assume I'm *with* anyone? "I'm on my own," I tell her. *What would it be like to be with her?*

"Care for company?"

It's as if she read my mind and offered what I've been wishing for. But I have a sudden glimpse of Cindy throwing herself at me to get that jock's attention. Is that the sort of invitation Rachel's making? I tell myself she's not like Cindy, and for a moment heat flares in my chest as if the air has caught on fire. Then I remind myself that I don't know what she's like, beyond a puzzle lover. I don't know if I'm just another puzzle she's picked up, or something more. I drop my eyes and shake my head, willing my heart to stop pounding.

"No." I know it sounds brusque, and I'm glad. I don't want her looking inside of me, calmly dissecting me. I can't let myself want that because it hurts too much when someone sees what I do (*what I am*) and pulls away.

"Why?"

She was expecting that, I realize. So I tell her a piece of the truth no one could understand without seeing my paintings. "You know too much about art."

But I see comprehension in her face before she turns away—she knows my art is who I am, and getting close to me would be the same thing as getting close to my paintings. Now she knows another piece of the puzzle that makes up me. I stare at the sketch pad and wonder how else I can screw up the evening. Maybe I should do this sketch another time. But I can see it in my mind so clearly—and I've never screwed up a drawing I could see like that.

I flip open the pad and uncap my pen, lowering it to the blank page. The lines take shape and the noise from the other kids disappears around me. There are only black lines on a creamy background, growing into Adrian's face. Not the way I thought I'd sketch him, trapping his prey. Not the way other people see him at all. Perhaps the way Adrian sees himself. I reach for that radiance I saw earlier. I've seen guarded hints of expression before (*love?*), but never so true as it was tonight after his quartet was performed so magnificently.

I seat him before a piano in the practice room he must have, like I have a studio. His look, focused on the black and ivory keys, carries the viewer's eye to the oversized music score, half completed and spread across the top of the piano. And the unfinished line of music leads the eye back to Adrian's face, and the luminous delight that fills it.

Then I'm finished. I glance over the whole, and wish I could paint this one. I'd like to use color to bring out the radiance. And it's more than a sketch—I draw what's true, but I paint what could be (*should be*) true. This is Adrian as he should be.

He'd read too much into a painting, though. He'll probably read too much into this. But I owe him, and I sign the drawing quickly before I can think about it too carefully. He'll get more pleasure out of this than anything else I could give him.

I tear the sketch out of the pad and stand up, feeling stiff. The ginger ale has gone flat. I realize that some of the kids have seen what I was drawing. I catch sight of a strange, sly sneer on some faces, but I turn away from them, the way I turned away from the kids who laughed at me for not playing Simon Says, the way I turned away from Cindy and Rob and the smirking middle school students. If I let other people's opinions tell me who I am, I'd have different paintings in me. And I'd never have drawn this sketch. Let them think what they like. All their opinions can do is remind me why I can't let anyone (*Rachel*) in.

Among the surrounding faces, I recognize Graeme Brandt—I hadn't seen him earlier. He's different tonight—more relaxed somehow, in an open-necked white shirt with long sleeves rolled up nearly to his elbows. There's a line of muscle in his forearm that I'd like to draw. Above the shirt collar, his expression is thoughtful, not sneering. I smile at him faintly before easing out of the row of seats and heading to the lobby in search of Adrian. I don't want to ask myself what Brandt thinks of the sketch.

Adrian looks up from an animated group conversation with a crowd (*wolf pack*) of kids I don't know (*and don't want to know*), and smiles at me even before I hand him the drawing.

"There—how do you like it?"

I see delight flare in his eyes before the color rises. It's easy to see that there's no flattery in the sketch. I can copy pompous stacks of books and spoiled fruit in my paintings, but I won't flatter someone untruthfully. What's the point of art if it's not true? And finding the right truth can show a greater kindness than playing games that only pretend to please.

A shadow crosses Adrian's face. "Is it for *Ventures*?"

I shake my head. "Just for you." At least, not for any more prying eyes than the ones here tonight who are busy drawing their own conclusions.

I turn away from his pleasure to get another ginger ale and see Graeme Brandt near the concession stand. He nods toward Adrian as I come up to him. "You drew him as he'd like to be seen, especially by you."

I shrug. "He did me a favor. I just wanted to repay it." He nods in silent agreement while I ask for the ginger ale. "You want a soda or anything?"

He shakes his head. "No, I'm fine." There's a relaxed quiet in his voice that wasn't there the other night.

Hemmed in by strangers, I search for something to say, some way to keep the conversation going so I can keep him beside me—keep him under observation for that *Ventures* sketch, I remind myself. But Graeme Brandt is as elusive as fleeting oil colors on water. I haven't even realized he's changed from peaceful to teasing before I hear the other guy's voice.

"All alone, Gray?"

Graeme grins. "Everyone I knew had other plans, it seems."

"So you've developed the artistic temperament," the student says to Graeme, and looks at me strangely. "I never noticed that side of you before."

"That's because you're a different type of artist."

This is the Graeme Brandt of the other night, not the one who looked into my sketch tonight, or the one who wrote that book.

An enormous clap of thunder heralds the rainstorm I felt blowing up earlier. A few kids jump, then laugh at themselves for their false fright. I wish suddenly that I could be far away from here, becoming part of the storm, but I can't begin to work out the vectors to plot an escape route through the shifting crowd. A burst of lightning flashes in overture to another explosion of thunder, and then the lights blink off.

6

Silence, except for the drumming of the rain. Then voices start, rising sharply as if they could drown out the darkness. I feel a hand take my arm and firmly pull me away from the center of the room to a window at the far side of the enclosed lobby. Beyond the glass the world is clear and bright in the intermittent flashes of lightning, and rain pounds the sidewalks and lawns, making them into alien ground for students and returning to them a wildness they lost long ago. Safe in the darkness, so near to the storm, I feel myself relax as I do only when I'm painting. The rushing water washes away the loneliness.

Long fingers of lightning reach out across the sky, turning the world a garish white, and in their light I look beside me to see who pulled me away from the room full of strangers. I half expect it to be Rachel. But I feel no surprise at seeing Graeme Brandt, standing tall and silent, both hands now in his pockets as the lightning illumines the planes of his face. Looking out over the storm, he makes me believe for an instant that he sees in it some of the things that I see. Perhaps he even sees something he wants to use in his work.

He glances at me briefly and smiles a clear, open smile—the first I've seen from him, and I smile back. Something between us is understood about the storm and the other kids and the party behind us. We've stepped out of Whitman. Silent, apart, we've somehow joined with the wild and raging force outside the window.

Minutes—hours—then the lights blink on again, blinding me, and I press against the glass, hopelessly straining to cut myself off from the false brightness indoors and to remain one with the storm. Not until Adrian appears at my side, gesturing to the now shadowy world beyond the glass pane, do I realize that Graeme Brandt has disappeared.

"Beautiful, isn't it?"

I nod, sorry that the distance between me and the storm is growing.

"The school has no sense of humor," Adrian tells me. "We've got to clear out, in case the power goes out again. Now there's logic for you—send us all out in the rain so we can get pneumonia, for fear of what we might do in the dark!"

I look around. The place has already mostly emptied. I blink, remembering why I was here in the first place. "I'm sorry—kind of a letdown for your big night."

"Not on your life!" Adrian declares. "I'd say the night was just about perfect."

I wince inside, not wanting to explore what I've let myself in for.

"Coming?"

The storm has eased to a drizzle. I can't see myself walking through the soft rain with Adrian. *With Rachel, perhaps? Or with Graeme...* But that's a wasted thought. I scramble for a way out. "Um, no. I think I'll go to my studio for a while."

"What do you plan to do there if the lights go off?"

I bite back a sharp retort. "Work on the still life, what else? It'll look better in the dark."

He laughs, if a little sadly. "Well, if you get stranded in the rain before reaching your safe haven, you can always dry off in two-oh-seven downstairs—that's my practice room. I always leave it unlocked."

I marvel at the confidence that casual comment implies. *Unlocked...* "Thanks," I tell him.

"Don't forget curfew," he warns.

"I won't." We have to sign in and out—dorm parents on guard. I watch Adrian go off with a few of the others, wait a few minutes, then head out with the last of the stragglers. I stand on the walk in front of the concert hall, feeling the clean wind and the cold drizzle on my face. It's raining harder than I thought, and I hunch my shoulders and wish I had a raincoat in my pack. The pack is waterproof for my sketch pad, but I'm getting soaked. I start walking, not knowing where I'm going.

"Want to share an umbrella?"

I look up, the rain plastering my hair to my head. There stands Graeme Brandt, jacketless, his white shirt gleaming faintly in the dark. I glance around—could he have been waiting for me? Standing in the rain with that umbrella, waiting for me to come out, knowing I'd come alone?

"Thanks." I feel like I've been thanking people all night.

He steps forward and the umbrella suddenly cuts off the rain on my face. "Where are you headed?"

I smile and shrug. "I don't know. I just felt like walking, but there's more rain than I expected."

He smiles back. "It's always better in the movies. Come on."

I walk beside him, surprised how easily we pace each other. With his height, I'd have expected to trot. He stays silent, and I remember he's a year older. He seems at once remote and infinitely enlightened. As we walk, the lamps that line the path sweep across his face, like headlights on the road. I can see one cheekbone lit for a few steps, then the corner of his mouth, then the shadows underneath his eyes are heightened. How would I paint him?

Suddenly he turns to me, catching my stare, and smiles easily. Without knowing why, I feel embarrassed at being caught, and look outside our umbrella world. I'm not sure where we are. I see a grassy stretch and a long, low building like a stable running along the side of the walk beyond the grass. I glance behind us.

"I thought you might like to see my studio," he says, his voice unexpectedly hesitant. "It was the closest place, and I figured you'd like to dry off." There's a trace of a question in his tone. I could say no, as simply as I told Adrian no, as firmly as I told Rachel no. But I told

Rachel I'd study Graeme Brandt and find a way to sketch him. I've seen something tonight, but I can't quite put it down on paper. It's cloudy, but it's there. *And if it's what let him write that book and get it published so the whole world could read it, then it's what I came to Whitman to find out.*

"Sure," I hear myself telling him. "I'd like that."

As we turn off puddled pavement onto muddy grass, sloshing side by side, a series of doors and windows comes into focus in the long, low building. I realize it's a row of studios, different from the building where I have mine. It must be a different arrangement for writers—or maybe it's a special perk for seniors. Graeme shifts the umbrella to his outside hand and fumbles between us for his keys. I hadn't realized how close to each other we were standing. Then he pushes the door open, reaches inside for a light switch, and gestures me through ahead of him.

A computer sits shrouded in a dustcover on an otherwise empty desk. The room isn't much larger than my studio, but it feels more like a room in a home—a wide recliner beside an end table with a lamp and enough space for a stack of papers, a hot plate beyond the computer, even a small refrigerator tucked under one side of the desk. Graeme ducks down and pulls out a ginger ale. "Is this your favorite? Unless you'd like something hot? I could fix some coffee or something."

I hang the strap of my pack over the doorknob, feeling suddenly like a kid with an adult. "Ginger ale's fine," I say, wondering how he knew. He hands it to me, and I fumble for something to say. "You hardly need a dorm room. You can practically live right here."

He smiles again, that easy, open smile he gave me earlier under the umbrella. "Sometimes I do." He moves the desk chair over and sits on it, pointing me to the recliner.

"I'm soaked."

"It'll dry." He waits for me to sit. "When I'm working on a book, I stay here for days at a time. I mean, I can eat here, work, even sleep on the recliner."

I feel the recliner's rough tweed enfolding me, and smile. This is what I'd been waiting for since I got here, for him to talk about his work. And that kind of dedication is what I wanted to hear. "I wondered just how an author goes about writing."

As he answers, I can hear an unmistakable affection for his work in his voice. "I don't know how other writers work, but it's more real for me than anything else. If I'm not here—if I'm at class, say, or in the dorm—the characters in the book get in the way. Dialogue comes alive in my head once I set up the situations, and I've got to be able to shut everything else out and just get it down on the computer, or in one of my notebooks. So I hide out here and write. My mentor worked things out with the dorm so they don't panic."

I feel a prickle of unease inside. It's almost like he's somehow reciting lines, but that can't be. This is the Graeme Brandt that I imagined, that I'd been looking for since I got to Whitman—the writer who loses himself in creating something extraordinary. And now I've found him. He writes brilliantly, and he lets everyone see what he writes, and he's not hounded by a baying wolf pack. He's even popular. Maybe he can tell me how I can do it, after all. Maybe I really *have* found where I belong.

I take a long swallow of the ginger ale and put the idea out of my mind that he's somehow performing these lines for me. He means them—they're real. He just knows how to express his feelings so well that it sounds like a script. Writers probably have that happen all the time. But what he's saying—it's something special, something true that he shares with me.

He's looking at me again, the way he looked at me in the storm, and I feel self-conscious again, inexplicably shy yet almost willing to open up to him. I start to ask him how he lives with people's expectations, how he writes the truth, knowing they won't like it. *How can I open up and still stay myself, and not be torn apart?*

"You're quite an artist." He breaks the silence before I can frame my words. "Have you ever thought of drawing yourself? You have a gift for capturing your subject's . . . soul."

I grin wryly, thinking of the back view for the auditions committee and the better Harlequin sketch hanging in my studio. "I did, but it was masked."

He looks surprised. "Why? You have a striking face— you shouldn't hide it."

"Ah, but it's a question of souls—"

Then I stop and feel the heat creeping up my neck. *So you've developed the artistic temperament,* that student had said in the concert hall. *I never noticed that*

112

side of you before. Finally I get it. I realize what Graeme Brandt's patient attention to me all night must mean. Stupid, stupid, not to see it sooner. I knew with Adrian from the start, but Graeme is more—what?—discreet. I remember the blond guy I saw come in with him at that Orientation Week party, and I think of the way Graeme looked at me after seeing that drawing of Adrian. God— he must think—

I fumble for a way to answer. "My...ex-girlfriend used to say that." I can't help it if my tone is forced.

He doesn't say anything for a moment, just studies my flushed face. "Why ex-? Just because you left for Whitman?"

It would be the easy way out, implying I've got tons of eager girlfriends missing me now that I'm at a new school. But I can't completely lie to those slivers of blue ice in his eyes. I choose my words carefully. "She decided she liked jocks better than artists with piles of oily"— I bite off the word *ugly* before it can escape, and finish lamely—"paintings."

His eyes never blink, but the ice softens. "I've found that guys can be a lot more dependable than girls. And they expect less." His voice is gentle and understanding, and I want to lean against it as I leaned into the wind before the storm and let down my guard—but I can't. I won't. Yet an aching emotion uncoils inside me, grieving that I'm betraying it.

I refuse to acknowledge it. Instead I look directly at Graeme. "Yeah, well, my policy since then has been to depend on nobody but me."

He doesn't say anything for a moment. Then he leans

back in the hard desk chair and clasps his hands behind his head. I look away from the curve of his bare arm and stare at the wall behind him. His voice is low. "Don't you get lonely?"

The need for friendship that has been hounding me all evening (*all my life*) cries out *Yes!* but my voice refuses to articulate the longing. "No. I've got my art."

"Is that always enough?" The blue eyes and the understanding in his tone draw me toward his face again.

No! But my shoulders shrug. "It has to be."

He nods easily and gets to his feet. "Want another ginger ale?"

I look down and realize the can is empty. I don't remember drinking it, but I must have. Dumbly, I shake my head. He smiles, as if amused.

"It's late," I explain awkwardly.

His smile disappears, and he asks quietly, "And you have to go?"

My sight blurs for a second, and I nod, not trusting my voice to explain how very much I do need to leave. He stands above me, not moving, and I see the pulse beat in the hollow of his throat.

"Do you really?"

His voice is an invitation to whatever I want (*another storm, or something else*), free from insistence or expectation. I struggle out of the recliner to my feet, ignoring the fact that he seems substantially taller than I am now, towering over me, where before we simply stood side by side.

"I have to go."

His face tells me that he hears the unsteadiness in my voice, that he suspects the feeling I refuse to confess, but he just takes the can from me, not commenting on the shock that passes between us as our hands touch. His eyes are still on my face, and I have to keep all my attention on not letting my own eyes betray me.

I fumble for my pack and am reaching to turn the doorknob when his voice stops me. "Good night, Charles."

The tone is warm, in spite of everything. It reminds me of the moments we shared in the brilliant lightning, of the walk through the rain together, of the dedication to his work that he so easily shared with me, as if we were friends already.

"Good night...Graeme."

The use of his first name is as great a confession of my feelings as I can manage, and I'm through the door and into the damp night before he can say anything more. Walking, sloshing through puddles, I try to think, but the images I've seen of Graeme Brandt spin dizzily in my head, refusing to merge, but still not fragments— a kaleidoscope whirl that slowly begins to take on a cloudy shape. I concentrate on the insight, trying to forget the feelings I betrayed, but the key to the insight seems to lie within the betrayal.

I feel I've walked miles and forded flooded streams by the time I reach the dorm in the late rain. I can't bear to face Adrian, but he's sound asleep. There's a note on the floor, slipped under the door by the dorm master, reminding me about curfews and asking me to see him in the morning. Big deal. If Graeme can "work things out" at his dorm, maybe his name can "work things out" for me. I stifle a giggle that sounds like a sob. The dorm master can figure out for himself why I was out late with Graeme Brandt in a thunderstorm.

I kick off my wet shoes and drop my soaked clothes on the floor. As I pull the covers over my head, images of Graeme Brandt flash in a kaleidoscope whirl, warning me that there's something else to him, something besides the easy closeness he offered me tonight. Exhausted, I reject the warning and the images and tune out the soft rumble of Adrian's snores. I tune out the whole world of Whitman High School and try to imagine myself back to my childhood bed, where I hugged my stuffed rabbit and dreamed of colored chalks and friends. But it's not a stuffed rabbit I want tonight. I long for something (*someone*) more than a friend in my bed, something more than a pillow to hold on to.

Excerpts from
Graeme Brandt's Journal

September 1 (Senior Year)

The traditional Orientation Week party last night—and what would they all say if they knew I wasn't working on anything? I went with Karl because he was expecting me to, but it's the last time. He's getting too obvious. Last year he knew how to be discreet, but apparently he had a wild summer. I'm not about to risk that. It's just—I need someone around when I'm not writing. I don't like to be by myself. If I could only start a new book, it would be okay. Then I'd have my characters. But without them, I need a person.

The party was okay. Everyone was eager to meet me, and I didn't really feel like a fraud—I mean, *The Eye of the Storm* really is a success, even if I never write another word. But I *want* to write something else....

I met someone unexpected. Not a writer, an artist. His name is Charles Weston. He's new, but he's not a freshman. I wonder why he came last night? There was a strange look in his eyes—he wanted something from me, I think. Actually, he has an extraordinary face. His features are very sharply drawn, in some places overdrawn, like the hollows of his cheekbones, and his skin is almost translucent, especially around the eyes, which fairly glitter in intensity when he focuses on someone. He seemed uncomfortable in the crowd, though, and held himself stiffly, like he wanted to avoid contact. I got the impression he was daring them all to try to reach him, yet at the same time hoping someone would.

He wanted to talk to me about my writing. He'd actually read my book. And there I was with Karl, who certainly hasn't read more than a page or two of it. Karl's a sculptor—reading isn't a required skill, I'm afraid, though working with blocks of stone and chunks of metal certainly gives him other assets in the muscle department.... What was I supposed to do? I turned the conversation around so I didn't have to give Charles a direct answer that would snub Karl and the others. But I could see he didn't like it. It was like he felt he deserved better of me. He seemed to take my book seriously and expected me to do the same. In public, no less.

But then I saw him at work. He went over to talk to Adrian Lawson for a while, and met Tyler Murdoch. And then he sketched him. Tyler, that is, not Adrian. Apparently he's going to be doing caricatures for *Ventures.* He was incredible. Right there, with everyone watching him, like it was a performance, he dashed off a searing sketch of Tyler—brutal, but totally honest.

While Charles was drawing, it was as if he retreated into another world, right there in the middle of the real world. The only way he seemed to acknowledge the kids around him was by making a big deal of his being left-handed, as though they were supposed to react to it somehow. A weird thing to feel self-conscious about. Why should he care? I wonder if someone said something cruel to him about it once, and he can't forget it? Or is it a symbol of something to him, somehow? But the way that left hand can draw! When he finished, he checked the sketch over to see if he was satisfied, then signed it with a bold, sweeping hand and presented it to Rachel Holland in front of everyone—rubbing Tyler's nose in it. Not that Tyler doesn't deserve it.

But I couldn't get away from the feeling that Charles wanted something from me. I went over to talk to him for a while, and the demand was in his tone of voice, in his eyes. He wanted to know what I was working on, and I didn't have an answer to give him. I guess he thought I was just putting him off because of the party. In a sense, I *was* putting him off. You don't talk seriously at parties, for a start. And I can't help this frustration—this fear—at not knowing myself what I'm going to write next. But there was no way Charles Weston could have known that.

Anyway, the texture of what he wanted was something different but something I couldn't identify enough to give him. On the surface, he projects an aggressive arrogance, but he wasn't like that with me. It was almost like he wanted some kind of alliance with me—but why? He doesn't even know me. It has something to do with the way he feels about my book.

Karl sure had some strong opinions on why, but he was just jealous. Could Charles be gay? He seemed to relax a little with Adrian. I feel an attraction that's more than just sexual, but I wonder if I could seduce him. Maybe that's what he wants, even if he doesn't realize it yet. I have to see him again.

October 2—late (Senior Year)

Charles Weston just left my studio. I have never wanted anyone so much. I saw him tonight at the party for the premiere of two new chamber works by students (one by Adrian). Charles was sketching in the concert hall when I saw him—not a vicious caricature like the one of Tyler. This time he was sketching Adrian, and I thought I understood, but now I'm completely at sea. He had captured the look of rapture on Adrian's face as he listens to his music, and no doubt as he looks at a lover as well. I looked at that sketch and thought I must be wasting my time trying to seduce Charles. There was too much insight, too gently drawn. When he gave Adrian the sketch, it looked like Adrian was floating off to heaven.

But Charles saw me when he finished drawing, and there was the same unstated demand, the same expectation I felt that first night. I could feel him drawn to me, as I was to him, and I could see he wasn't sure how to carry on a conversation after our failure last time. I'd done some checking on him, after seeing that sketch he did of Tyler—the art department is buzzing about him because no one has seen what he paints. Apparently he grudgingly showed the auditions committee the minimum number of paintings he could get away with to be accepted here. Then he shipped crates that are supposed to be full of paintings to his studio, but has never let anybody in to see them. I wasn't sure whether he just liked being mysterious to get attention, or whether he had some other reason for hiding his work—any more than I could see clearly what he wanted from me. But then there was the storm.

The electricity went out, and there were plenty of shrieks and giggles in the dark, and then the storm exploded outside the windows. It was a stunning electric storm, and the room full of other people faded until Charles and I were alone, and there wasn't any need to search for something to say to each other. I knew exactly what he wanted. I drew him to the window and watched him stare at the sky, bathed in the cold lightning flashes that split the dark. Then he looked at me and smiled, and I felt the world turn inside out within me.

After the lights came back on, I managed to charm an umbrella off of one of the stagehands who remembered me from when I hung out with Ben's friends, and I waited outside for Charles. It was still raining when he left, a steady drizzle that made him glad for the umbrella. I could feel him looking at me under the lampposts as we walked, studying me, wanting something more. And I thought I knew what it was. I got him to come to my studio, but he wouldn't stay. God knows I wanted him to.

He asked me again about my work. In my studio I could finally answer him in the words he wanted to hear, even if I couldn't tell him what he seemed to want most—that I was writing a new book. I'm not even writing any new stories; I got so sick of the ideas I had starting strong and then dissolving into nothing but the same old story told over and over. But I didn't have to tell Charles that. I could talk about the way it felt when the book was actually working and I got lost in it. The bond we had forged under the lightning translated our words into more than just sounds, and I could feel him reaching out to me again.

Part of him fled when I reached back. I still don't completely understand why. He's been trying to make a connection with me since he came here—he clearly wants more than a casual friendship.

I could tell I'd spooked him, and I tried to draw him closer again, but it was as if he'd split himself, half-wanting, half-frightened. I tried to back off to give him a safe distance, but by then there was no way to bring him back. He had to go, he wanted to stay, and he finally escaped into the night again.

What was it he really wanted? I thought I understood. I'd have given him whatever he asked for, if I only knew what he was asking. I'm not sure he understands, himself. I only wanted to please him—I could do that without sex.

I feel drained. Actually, I think I'd almost prefer a relationship without sex. Sometimes the memory of sleeping with Karl just bores me. I'd rather offer Charles whatever closeness he wants, just to feel as alive as I felt tonight.

Why does he show such interest in my writing? What does he expect of me? I can see how serious he is about his art, though I can't understand why he keeps his paintings locked away in his studio. He demands the same absolute seriousness about my writing that he feels about his art, and I can give him that.

But there's something more he's looking for. I can't see it yet. I only know I want him—on whatever terms he sets. But if he insists that I write this next book he keeps asking about, I don't know what I can do. I still can't find a new book within myself. Why am I drifting? What am I going to do?

7

"You do understand the importance of the curfew, Charles?" Mr. Pullton asks, his face a mask of regret and concern.

Oh, yeah—you want to make sure what almost happened last night doesn't happen. "Of course, sir. But the storm kind of changed things." *A lot of things.*

"Yes, you were at the premiere last night?" He sounds more relaxed, now that he's on safer ground.

"That's right. They made us leave after the power came back on, but it was still raining pretty hard."

"Your roommate got back in time."

"Well, I didn't." *Can't lose my temper—he can probably ground me, or expel me.* I try to explain, "I got pretty wet, and Graeme Brandt suggested I wait out the rain in his studio." The kaleidoscope of images still spins in my head, but I try to ignore it.

"I see." He looks like he can't decide if he's relieved or suspicious. Fair enough.

"I'm doing a series of sketches of seniors for *Ventures,*" I tell him. "Rachel Holland asked me to get to know Graeme Brandt and sketch him, so we started talking at the party."

Now he nods, satisfied. And I feel like a cockroach in a paper hat, all dressed up to look pretty so people will ooh and aah, instead of recoiling at the multitude of lies and half-truths I'm telling.

"In the future, just try to keep an eye on the time, Charles." He smiles. I think he's trying to look kind. "We're not jailers here, you know. But I'm trying to stand in for your parents while you're at Whitman."

Mother says... be a good boy. Like my parents would have a clue about what happened last night. I look appropriately appreciative at the father surrogate—*Thank you, Daddy*—and he releases me to go to class.

≡

Introductory Programming blurs with *Lord Jim* from English class. For my term project, could I write an interactive game program that puts the student in Jim's situation? He'd have to decide which one of Jim's false images to play so that he can win in the end. Could I create a kaleidoscope program to do that? Would it be possible? Can you win in the end?

"Where's your disc, Weston? You're not paying attention."

Mother says... be polite. "Sorry, Ms. Cooper. I've got it in—" Chuckles erupt around me as I struggle to eject the compact disc.

The girl beside me leans over, her long black braid dangling in the aisle between us. "Try dragging it to the trash," she advises.

I ram the mouse to move the cursor up to the circular icon and click on it, then drag it down to the trash and release it. The machine makes a grating noise, and I wish savagely for an onslaught of electronic cats devouring computer mice, until the tray jumps out at me.

Ms. Cooper takes the disc, shaking her head. I don't think I saved anything on it, so she doesn't know the half of it yet.

I glance at the girl who rescued me. "Thanks, ah—"

"Alona," she supplies, helpfully. "I'm Alona. And you're Charles, right?" She grins at me.

I nod and dredge up a smile for her. "Thanks, Alona."

"No problem, Charles."

I can't face lunch, so I head to Still Life early. The fruit is in the refrigerator, but I don't need it. The painting is actually done. I don't know why I'm here. I lift off the drape and stare at it, a pathetic bowl of used up fruit, as fake and flat as Mr. Wallace.

Without really asking myself what I'm doing, I lift a tube of chromium yellow from the easel tray and open it. I'm only thinking about acrylics, not about painting anything with them right now. I prefer oils, but Mr. Wallace has us do still lifes in acrylics. He says it's easier to paint over something to make changes with acrylics—a better paint form for teaching. Erasers for the would-be artist to re-make the image at will.

Now there's titanium white on my palette as well, and black, and my brush is mixing, looking for just that right luminous hint of light hitting the lumpy rind— the same angle of light that washes out the lifeless bowl of fruit. It takes shape nicely on the canvas. *Mr. Wallace says . . . paint what you see . . . This is what I see.* Delicate strokes, pinpoint dabs—and there it lies, brighter and more real than anything else in the arrangement. I must have known it would go there from the start—the composition was unbalanced without it. I had placed the bowl of fruit too far to the right. The front left-hand corner of the table was crying out for something—for this.

Suddenly I hear footsteps and voices in the hall— class is about to start. I blink at the canvas, surprised but pleased. And at ease, suddenly, after the uneasy night and the lousy morning. No spinning impressions, no confusion, just a clean, true image. Truer for never having existed in Mr. Wallace's stillborn version of life.

I hang the drape loosely over the drying paint and am at the sink washing my brushes when the first students arrive. They ignore me. I think one of the reasons my parents let me come to Whitman was that they thought I'd make friends here, even if those friends were just other artsy types like me. Only they're not like me. They want to please the Mr. Wallaces, and I don't.

He ceremoniously sets out the bowl of fruit and reminds us that our finished pictures are due by the end of class. I leave my painting draped and pull out my sketch pad. Now that my mind is clear, there's something about that kaleidoscope concept I want to try to put on paper.

"Not working today, Mr. Weston?"

What does it look like I'm doing? Of course, I'm working. I look up at him. "It's finished, sir."

"Well, then, let's have a look at it."

I glance around at the other students, but they're not allies. Some of them concentrate on their own paintings, but others look eager to see what he'll say about me this time. Suddenly the good feeling I had dissolves. I shouldn't have done it. I should paint it out. The acrylics will cover it.

"Actually, sir, I think I'd like to do a little more first."

"Fine, Mr. Weston. Let's see if I can help you with those finishing touches."

"Sir—" But it's too late. He's lifted the drape between his bony forefinger and thumb. And I don't want to paint it out. I wish I hadn't added it, but I'm also glad I did. It transforms a sophomoric study into a painting.

He turns to me, his thick brows drawn together in either anger or surprise. Probably both. "What is that?"

I swallow. "It's a lemon, sir."

The class erupts in laughter. Fine. I don't mind being comic. They're the apples and oranges and pears, but I'm the lemon in their happy little bowl of fruit. It's the only life in the painting—the way the pears are bruised, you can see they're dead, used up, but that lemon glows with life.

Mr. Wallace rips the drape off my canvas and hurls it to the floor. "There is no lemon in that still life, Mr. Weston! Was this something else *you thought* was missing?"

I look at him, knowing anything I say will be the wrong answer.

Simon says... apologize. Redo it.

"Do it over, Mr. Weston!" he says. "And you will receive a mark off for turning it in late."

"No sir."

Before he can do more than stare at me in stunned amazement, I reach into my easel tray for the knife I use to trim my brushes. I dig it into the canvas, just below the top stretcher bar. A girl gasps (shock or delight?) somewhere behind me, and I slice straight across the bar to the right-hand side. Then I slice down the side, about three-quarters of the way. Holding the upper right corner, I carefully slice just beneath the edge of the painted table, below the fruit arrangement, stopping just short of my lemon. I pull the loose flap of canvas taut, and slowly cut my way up to the top. The lemon hangs in the lower left-hand corner of the shreds of my original painting, but the bowl of fruit, now neatly centered in a smaller rectangle of canvas, flops loosely.

"Here, Mr. Wallace." I drop the knife back into my easel tray and shove the still life at him. "Here's your assignment. On time, and nothing more than you asked for." *Nothing more—no art, no creativity, just a copyist job.* That's all he wants.

Mr. Wallace grips the limp canvas—I can see a cluster of grapes crushed under his bony fingers—and glares at me. "Get out."

"Yes sir."

I jam my sketch pad back in my pack and leave. Rachel said to tell Mr. Brooks if things got too bad, but he'll just side with Mr. Wallace—they're both adults. They think they know everything, but they've forgotten it all, instead.

In my studio, staring at my night skyscape surrounded by razor-sharp buildings, I wonder if he'll flunk me. It would be hard to justify on the basis of that "perfect" still life, but maybe he could flunk me for general insubordination. Is that grounds for expulsion at Whitman?

The buildings on the canvas surround the shimmering stars and reflect their light back, and I suddenly straighten up and stare inside the painting at the glaring reflections. A different sort of mirror takes shape in my mind as the pieces of the puzzle that have been spinning in confusion settle into a pattern at last. Is this pattern what I was warning myself about the night of the storm? Is this really Graeme Brandt? Not the image I'd hoped to find, but the truth inside?

8

I have to draw Graeme. I have to see if I'm right about him. I'm not sure I like the image, but I can't get it out of my mind. I'll know as soon as I see him and put the lines on paper whether it's a true drawing or not. And I have to know—I have to understand him. I want to startle him, also. I want to define the bond between us. Or maybe I want to break it.

The drama department has a collection of one-acts scheduled next weekend, with a cast party after. If I'm right, that's the sort of party Graeme won't miss.

"You going to the cast party?" I ask Adrian.

"Probably," he says, a secretive smile on his face. I wonder who he's going with, glad that he's got a date.

"Can you get me in?"

"You don't really need an invite," he tells me, his voice curious. "But you can tag along with me if you like."

"Thanks." Graeme has to be there.

"What's so important about this party, anyway?"

I shrug. "I'm just a party animal, I guess."

Adrian laughs, a brittle sound like breaking glass. "Oh, that's you, all right!" The sketch I made of him hangs above his desk. I'm touched, and a little sorry I drew it for him, because I suspect he puts more stock in the gift than he should. But it's a true drawing, even if it's only one side of him.

I make it through the week, painting and keeping my mouth shut in Mr. Wallace's class. The shreds of the lemon are gone the next class session, and he never says anything else about it. Stalemate, I guess. We have a new arrangement—a tumble of children's building blocks. I like the angles and the shadows and use charcoal to rough in the blocks on a fresh canvas without any little extras.

I wonder what Mr. Wallace would say if I painted the whole thing in black and white, or maybe sepia tones, like an old photograph? But I don't, because I suddenly see that my perspective on these hard-edged cubes isn't quite perfect. I rub out the charcoal and adjust an angle slightly, looking at the blocks in a different way—looking at the idea of fundamental techniques in a different way. If I'd seen the lines like this in my painting of the roof, the image would have been sharper, more focused. Why couldn't Mr. Wallace show us that, instead of getting so hung up on the purity of photo-painting his dead-life arrangements? Or is that what he's been trying to teach us, and I haven't been paying attention? I paint the blocks with care.

I start phoning the people Rachel wants me to sketch, asking if I can come by and watch them work sometime, explaining that I don't want them to "sit" for me, just be themselves, and I'll take care of the rest. It sounds so simple.... They fall for it, of course, and I start sketching the truth they never realize they've revealed. I'm on overdrive, filling every minute so I don't have to think.

I even nerve myself to talk to Alona again in computer class. I ask her some questions about the kaleidoscope idea I had for the *Lord Jim* false image game, and she flips back her long braid and lights up with excitement. She goes on about if-then cause-and-effect logic strings. I picture shimmering strands of gray brain matter logically stretching from situation to image, but don't think this will help me write the program, until Alona suggests we work together on it. Apparently Ms. Cooper said we could team up for the term project. I must not have been listening. Alona says she couldn't think of anything interesting enough, but she likes this because she's a writer. I don't let her see my inner wince at the word *writer. Are all writers like Graeme? Do they fit the pattern I've seen for him?* I don't know Alona well enough to know what she's like, and I don't think I want to. I like the way she smiles, though, and I don't want to see her eyes slide away from me (*from my paintings*) uncomfortably. I don't want to let myself hope they might not slide away but will light up with pleasure. It hurts more when I let myself hope.

Finally time drags past and gets me to the night of the one-acts, and I sit through them numbly, waiting. Bits of plays, moments of theater, fragments flickering onstage, and all I can think of is the images of Graeme Brandt in my mind's kaleidoscope.

This party isn't at the theater. The director's one of the dorm masters, and he's throwing the cast party in his dorm apartment. I wander in behind Adrian and a light designer from the one-acts, as if I belong, and nobody stops me. A few faces smile at me—they look dimly familiar from the party after Adrian's quartet last week. If the same students are here, then I'm right that this is the group he feels comfortable with—I'm right that he'll come, too. *Graeme.* I hunt through the ice chest, hoping for a ginger ale, find one, and wait for him.

As soon as he walks through the door, I can't help my mind flying to his. But he's not alone tonight. He comes in talking to one of the actors, a few steps behind an older man who looks familiar. I saw him at the Orientation Week party. He has a strong, wary face, and Graeme keeps glancing at him, including him in the conversation. I watch them together, testing the image that haunts me.

Graeme glances across the room and our eyes meet. He flashes the same clear smile I remember too well from the other night. When I don't respond right away he raises his eyebrows slightly, and I realize I have responded. I'm smiling back at him without meaning to.

He says something to the others and crosses the room toward me. The actor shrugs and heads off to the kitchen, but the man trails Graeme possessively, his sharp black eyes examining me narrowly. I wouldn't like to tangle with him.

"Charles. How're you doing?"

The tone is warm but makes no demands, with none

of the closeness I backed away from before. I feel relieved—almost safe being friendly with him.

"Fine. Good show, wasn't it?" *Was it? I have no idea.*

"We'll have to wait to see what Tyler writes about it before we know about that," he returns, his voice now rippling in amusement. The right tone for the party. "This is Mr. Adler, my mentor." And then his tone changes again. "Sir, this is Charles Weston, the new sketch artist for *Ventures*. He just transferred here."

"Welcome to Whitman," Mr. Adler tells me. He glances around. "Don't make too late a night of it, Gray. You should be working."

Graeme smiles at him gently. "Yes sir. As soon as the new book's right in my mind, I'll get to work like a good boy. You'll be begging me to take some time off and go to a party before I burn out."

Mr. Adler sighs. "At least you've got something in the works. It's been a long time since that first book, Gray."

"I know."

Mr. Adler shakes his head, then glances around for the director. "I'm going to see if Bill needs a hand."

Graeme watches him go. "He's right, of course."

I nod. "I've been asking about your next book since I met you. At least you *have* to answer to him. I'm glad something's coming into focus."

He smiles faintly. "It isn't. But it doesn't hurt him to think it is."

I can't answer that. The silence lengthens between us until it becomes dangerous, but all I can think is, *I'm right—I know how to draw him.*

"Hello, Charles. Graeme." Rachel's cool voice breaks

the silence, and I can't quite hide the relief as I turn to her. Shared silence means understanding, and Graeme and I don't really understand each other. It means acceptance (*even belonging*)—things I can't be part of, no matter how much I want to. I thought he could show me how to belong without playing games, but he can't.

"Hi," I tell her.

"Any luck setting up appointments with the students I suggested?" she asks, her thumbs hooked in the pockets of a paisley vest that looks like swirls of oils on a watery surface. Graeme glances at me quizzically.

"I'm doing some sketches to go with an article," I tell him. "Yeah, I've met with three of them already and seen their work. I've already done roughs."

"Good—I'd like the lot by next week."

"I think I can manage that."

Graeme says, "I'll let you guys talk shop." He gives me another smile and heads across the room.

Rachel watches his graceful walk, then turns back to me. "What about him?"

I tell her, "I was planning to do a rough sketch tonight, but I think I know just what to draw."

Her smile matches my own, and without warning time slides to a halt. *I know all about Graeme Brandt, I want to tell her. I know about all of them—the insiders, the successes that everyone else looks up to because they feel safe with them. I see what they think they are, and I understand why people like them. And I can tell you because you're not like them, are you? You're like me.*

Then I see answering delight flare in her eyes, and I blink back into myself, remembering that she's not like

135

me, not in the end. *Why not? Why shouldn't she be like me? Why shouldn't* someone *be like me?* But that's only wishful thinking. It's just that I *want* her (*someone*) to be like me. The real Rachel wants to see inside of me and rearrange the pieces, and that's different from what I do—I arrange the pieces in my sketches so other people can see the pattern. Rearranging pieces is more like forcing your pattern on someone else.

Nobody's like me, in the end. I just have to find a way to get used to it. I slide my sketch pad out of my pack and turn away, looking for a place to sit. I don't care how rude she thinks I am—the ruder, the better.

A mahogany telephone table stands in a corner, and I close in on it, pulling out the straight-backed chair and moving the notepad, the mug of pens and pencils, and the little vase of silk flowers to make room to draw. I deliberately don't look back toward Rachel. I pull out my sketch pad and make myself think of Graeme, instead. There's the deferential student I saw with his mentor tonight, the celebrity I saw at the writers' party that first week, the charmer I saw in action after the concert, the aloof romantic who watched the storm with me, the writer I saw in his studio, the intimate friend I pushed away. The images revolve around and around inside my head as the kaleidoscope races out of control—all of them Graeme, and none of them the *real* Graeme.

My pen moves across the sketch pad, but my unruly left hand seems to have a mind of its own. Instead of the shifting lines of Graeme's (*beautiful*) responsive face, my hand produces a strong face framed by a neat cap of shining hair, clear eyes, with highlights in them that break apart into shifting kaleidoscope shards of colored glass. Before the lines of Rachel's face can come into focus, I turn over the page and force my hand to follow my eyes across the room to Graeme Brandt.

He stands talking to his mentor, the perfect posture of respect. His expression is attentive, and even though I can't hear his voice I'm sure it's just the right tone for a student accepting his teacher's advice. It's a terrific performance, better than anything onstage tonight. *Adrian says . . . show time.*

Now I start sketching in earnest—swift uncompromising lines, unyielding black. All the thought I've put into seeing inside of Graeme, all my struggles to understand him, everything I hoped and the truth I have to face—it all goes into the drawing. A slender figure emerges, pen poised in his graceful right hand. Around the figure, a series of mirrors reflect wished-for images toward the waiting author. I take pains to show each expectation. But within the circle of mirrors, and above the lean body, just where the head should be, I draw yet another mirror—huge, empty, all-encompassing, reflecting all of the images back on themselves. Without hesitation, ignoring the ache in my fingers that tells me I've grasped my pen too tightly for too long, I sign the sketch and rip it out of the pad. I know it's a true drawing.

I hear a gasp and a distant murmur of voices. I mean to look for Rachel, to give her the sketch, but when I look up I see Graeme coming toward me, his expression puzzled but friendly. *I know,* I want to tell him. *You see? I understand now. I've seen how you play the game. But*

I don't understand why—and I don't think I can forgive you for not being who I thought you were.

On a deeper level, I'm begging, *Please let me be wrong.*

He reaches the table and bends down to look at the drawing, then freezes, staring at it. I wait for him to say something, but he looks up from it, his blue eyes gone nearly black, turned into bottomless pools. Someone says something to him, and he snatches up the paper, folding it roughly in half to hide the stark lines.

"Graeme—" I can't shorten his name, like the others do, the ones who don't know him. But he doesn't stop to listen. He backs away from me, then turns. He's across the room and gone before I have the chance to say more.

"Well, well."

The other kids, strangers with hungry eyes who enjoyed the show, have turned away, whispering to each other. But Adrian leans against the wall beside the small table.

"Your sketch seems to have made quite a stir."

His tone sounds almost relieved at Graeme's abrupt departure, and he studies the door instead of meeting my eyes. I realize he's been standing there for a while now—long enough to have seen the sketch before Graeme hid it—long enough to compare it with the sketch I did of him—no doubt long enough to tell himself that he's made a conquest after all, that he won me over to the point where I've spurned Graeme Brandt for Adrian Lawson. Something inside of me snaps at his assumption that I could care enough about him to be intentionally kind to him and deliberately cruel to Graeme. I want to rip the sketch I made of him into shreds. Why did I ever think that *roommate* might mean *friend*? That his music that night might mean we had something in common? You let somebody get a little close to you, and they think they own the right to twist your actions any way they like. Adrian turns to me and his eyes widen, nonplussed by the fury he sees in mine.

I hear a snicker and snap my head around. The guy's face is dimly familiar—someone from the concert party, maybe? Some stranger who doesn't know me, doesn't matter, but who must be drawing the same conclusion as Adrian? The other student meets my eyes for only a second, then he lifts his shoulders in the barest shrug and turns away.

I grab my sketch pad, shove it into my backpack, and get to my feet, leaving Adrian to hold up the walls on his own. Why do I keep forgetting? Why do I let anyone get close? Rachel stands there, gazing at me with such understanding and regret that I want to scream at her for asking me to draw Graeme if she knew what he was like. I want to scream at Adrian, at all of them. But mostly at her. She has no right to feel for me, no right to realize what I put into that sketch, no right to sense how I feel about Graeme (*and about her—to sense how much I wish she could be like me—how much I wish she could actually know me and like me, but she can't*), no right to look at me through those cool eyes and break me into fragments and *see inside me.*

I force my shaking legs to walk past her. I want to grip her in my left hand and shake her until she loses

139

that look of understanding, until I shake that knowledge from her brain and her eyes turn blind and meaningless like everyone else's (*Graeme's*) eyes.

Then I'm out in the steamy night, and I don't know where to go. I can't face my room, with Adrian coming back to it later. I can't think about him or I'll end up wanting to shake him as violently as I want to shake Rachel. I can't think about any of them.

My feet are moving across cracked, uneven concrete sidewalks. I'm out of the dorm area and into the main campus. I don't care about the curfew. I don't care about Whitman. I only came here for Graeme. And that's destroyed, or what I thought I'd find there never existed. I don't belong here, anyway.

Then I realize I'm heading for the studio building. I can lock myself in my studio and paint out all of them.

Excerpts from
Graeme Brandt's Journal

October 9—late (Senior Year)

He drew me. For some reason, I thought I'd be exempt, and yet...it wasn't a caricature like before. There was no malice in it, like Tyler's. There sure wasn't any love, either, like the one he drew for Adrian. Why? What did he mean?

He drew me as a mirror, reflecting other mirrors in a grotesque dance that whirls on forever. Sure I mirror what people expect sometimes—he does the same himself. Or he deliberately acts opposite to what people expect—that's just a backward reflection. Everyone reflects people's expectations—I learned that a long time ago. That's why I wrote *The Eye of the Storm,* to show that. But that's not *all* a person is. That's not all *I* am. Mr. Adler wanted to know what was going on, but I couldn't show him the sketch. He'd never have understood. No one would understand.

I don't understand.

Why did he single out that one aspect of me from all the others? I'm more than a reflection. But being that reflection *sometimes* means that people leave me alone when I want to do something that really matters. Isn't that how it works? We all reflect what people want us to be when we want to please them, but we're also more than just reflections of anything outside us. Aren't we? And yet...

I remember one day before I came to Whitman. My dad picked me up after work. I think maybe I'd gone to the library or something, and he came by to drive me home. It was a crisp fall evening, and Dad drove slowly, with the windows rolled down to feel the cool air. I could catch the tart smell of leaves burning.

Dad wanted to talk to me. He started out by talking about his job, clenching the steering wheel firmly with both hands, staring deliberately out through the windshield rather than at me. He said I should know that things hadn't been going as well as he'd hoped they would at the bank, that one of the other executives there was making some sort of trouble for him. I never understood what exactly, and he didn't want to say. What he wanted to tell me was that things were on their way to getting better. He said he didn't really understand my writing, but he was proud of me, proud that I'd been accepted at Whitman. He was proud that he could afford to send me, too. And I shouldn't tell Mom because it was a big secret, but he was saving money so he could take her to Florida for a second honeymoon. She always talked about wanting to go to Florida.

I could feel that he wanted something from me, the way Charles wanted something. But I knew what Dad wanted. Mom always said how hard Dad worked, all for us, so we had to let him know we appreciated it and we believed in him. I knew what Dad wanted was for me to confirm that he was just what a father should be—hardworking and good. He wanted me to look up to him and respect him, the way Mom always praises him, so I did it. I nodded at him and told him how glad I was that he was my dad, and that I'd make him proud of me, as proud as I was of him—all the lines I knew he wanted to hear. By the time we got home, he was in a great mood, joking with Mom during dinner.

And he kept looking at me like we'd been through something big together.

I knew he wanted to be the respected father to the admiring son, a television dad from the old days. And I became that son—I gave him what he wanted. It was so easy. And it didn't hurt me any. That part of your drawing is true enough, Charles—right then, I was a mirror of his expectations. And it made him happy.

We all reflect other people's expectations back at them. That's what I wrote about—the way we all do it in order to get something that's really important to us. Alan Travis wanted to save his family, and he'd show anyone whatever they expected to see in order to succeed at that. So what if I do the same thing—reflect people's expectations back at them to make them feel better, or to make them like me, or help me, so that I can do what I really want? Why didn't you draw that, Charles, draw what I really want, who I *really* am? Why didn't you draw *me* in that central mirror?

It's like you didn't think I was there, inside the mirror, but I am—I have to be. Or else there's nothing inside any of us, just a blank surface waiting to reflect something, and that can't be. It just can't! But—I was there with my dad, only I wasn't. I said what he wanted to hear. I didn't tell him what I really thought of him as a dad, because I didn't really think of him at all. I didn't have to.

Was I only real in the way I reflected what he expected to see in me back to him? And was his image made real because I reflected it back to its source? Two mirrors, constantly assuring each other of something that should have been true, and might have had a chance to *be* true, only we insisted on accepting images, instead. Why is that, Charles? Do you know? Do you have the answer?

Or did you see more than you thought? Did you see the emptiness I've felt inside myself, and draw that? Was that what you were trying to show me, Charles? Can you tell me what that emptiness is, and how to fill it?

I've got to talk to you.

9

Bolts of cadmium red banging on my studio door. It doesn't matter—the hasp lock is in place. Nothing can get inside. Nothing except color and noise.

"Charles! Open the door!"

Brown tones, streaked with yellow pain. Who would cry out to me like that? Time disappeared—did I miss a class? Has Adrian come to hunt me down? Is that part of being the experienced roommate? *Adrian says . . . go to class.* No, not anymore, not just the experienced roommate, the thwarted—what? Why did I sketch him? *Charles says . . . stay alone.*

"Open up, damn it! It's Graeme."

Graeme says . . . open up and let me get closer, let me get inside you, let me—

"Charles!"

If I never open the door he'll have to go away, won't he? I don't want Graeme. I don't want any of them.

"Charles—I've *got* to talk to you!"

His voice is urgent, almost angry. I want to keep the door locked, but I can't turn him away. I hurt him last night, and now I owe him. I owe Adrian. I owe— I drop my brushes into turpentine to keep them soft and just leave my palette. Graeme looked so shocked last night.... Why did I agree to sketch him in the first place?

"Please, Charles—"

I open the door, and we stare at each other. His brows are drawn together and his eyes are ice crystals, but then his face changes. Not a mirror, maybe—should I have chosen putty, instead?

"Are you okay?" Now his voice is gentle, caring. Why should he care? If he's so angry with me, why can't the anger be a wall between us?

I step into the hallway and shut my door, sliding the hasp lock into place. I can build the wall again, if I don't look at him. "You come here," I tell him, "you beat on my door in a rage, and the instant you see me you change character. You drop all your own anger in your rush to become what I want you to be." My voice cracks as I confess that much, at least. "Don't you ever get tired of reflecting other people? How can you stand yourself? What *are* you in an empty room?"

My voice has risen, and I hear a smothered laugh from down the hall as the anger floods back into Graeme's face. I glance at the corridor, then to the stairwell. More strangers mired in their wrong assumptions.

"There's got to be somewhere we can talk," he says in a low voice.

He looks at my locked door, but I'd rather have the whole school hear the argument than take him inside my studio. Wordlessly I lead the way up the polished stone stairs to the roof, and step out into a soft, clear morning. Perhaps the monsoons are over at last.

"Well?" I keep my voice hard. I can do that much. "What did you want to say?"

Gravel crunches as he strides across the roof to the parapet where I'm standing. I turn and he raises a clenched fist. I almost wish he would hit me—smashing whatever lies between us and proving to me finally that we're nothing alike. Then his fist opens and a crumpled piece of paper drifts down to the gravel at my feet. It's my sketch.

Weary beyond fighting, I slide down the parapet siding to sit on the sharp edges of gravel. I reach out to smooth the wrinkled paper. Graeme eases himself down to sit cross-legged, and we stare at the drawing, neither of us ready to look up.

"How could you draw me like that?" Graeme says finally. He points at the kaleidoscope of mirrors glaring up from the paper. "How could you see that?"

I see him sitting beside me, close enough to touch. I see the Graeme Brandt who swept into the writers' party, the Graeme Brandt who turned one face to the storm, another to the jealous student after the concert, and still another to me later that same night, the Graeme Brandt who wrote a book that captured me with its honesty about how people live the expectations of others. He's one person beside me, vulnerable now (*wanting to get close to me*), but he's a kaleidoscope of all those Graemes at the same time. I don't know whether to shout at him or cry. I wanted him to be such a different person.

"How can you be so surprised? You see everybody around you—can't you see yourself?" Now that I've started I rush headlong, saying all the things I'd only half dared to think since I stood in his studio. "You're nothing but a lifeless mirror that reflects everyone's expectations! Your book reflects that empty mirror—your characters are just reflecting all the other blank lives around them. I thought you were warning people about not living like that—not just showing them how to do it because that's all you know!"

I follow the words, not even knowing where they're leading me, only knowing they're true, as true as the drawing I made. "That kind of existence isn't really life—not unless all you want to be is a reflection of the mediocrity all around you. And if you wrote that book, you can't be mediocre." *But if he's not, then—*

Of course he couldn't show me how to be myself, how to escape the people who want to play Simon Says. Graeme was always the master player, himself. I just hadn't wanted to admit it. He wasn't writing any sort of warning of how terrible the world could become if you pushed the idea of living up to someone else's expectations too far. He was just writing what he thought everyone was, because that's what he was himself. I look up at him, putting my heartsick realization into words. "You're dead, Graeme. You're nothing but the reflection of all the empty expectations around you. How could you write that book and not see that Alan was you?"

He stares at me in horrified silence, and I realize he didn't understand what he had done. Above us, a bird darts past, toward the trees, screaming a hoarse cry.

"You're dead, inside, where you should be most alive," I say softly, "and you didn't know."

I thought he did it on purpose. I thought he'd killed his inner self, knowing what he was doing the way I know when I hide my inner self, disguising my art as sketches so I can deal with people without suffering the pain of their rejection. But for once his expression doesn't seem to be a reflection of anything except his own inner emptiness. His eyes deaden, and his face goes slack and hollow. He sits motionless, only the breeze ruffling his thick black hair. I should have known better. It's his *life*— It's not his fault I wanted him to be someone different. That was only *my* expectation, after all. I lean forward and reach across to him.

"Graeme?"

Color comes back into his face so slowly that it takes me a while to realize he'd gone deadly white. As he comes back to himself, Graeme focuses on me. He squeezes his eyes shut and flinches, just for a moment, before he gets control of himself. Then he sits motionless, every muscle taut, with my hand lying there on his arm.

"Graeme?"

His eyes open, flicker to mine, then drop to the sketch. He takes a sudden gasping breath, and then looks at me again.

"Yes. I'm fine now." He nods jerkily. "Yes. It's okay."

I grip his arm, and he shudders convulsively.

"I—" His voice chokes off and he shuts his eyes tightly. "Charles...what about all the others?" I have to strain to hear him. "Aren't they mirrors in their own way? Who isn't a reflection of what the world around

149

him expects, in the end? There's nothing...unnatural about it."

The wolf pack is made up of mirrors, wanting everyone else to be nothing but a mirror, too. But an artist (*and aren't we all artists?*) should be something more. I grope for words to explain. "Where does a reflection start? Who begins it? There has to be a source that doesn't live up to any expectation from anyone else, just itself."

Graeme opens his eyes. "Maybe there aren't any sources anymore. Maybe we're just living up to what's been done and seen and believed for so long that it's all there is."

I don't say anything, and he smiles a little. "No. You don't think so, do you?" He glances at the crumpled sketch. "Okay then—what about you, Charles? Don't you do the same thing?" His stumbling words gain strength. "You see yourself as an artist, right? But you keep your paintings locked up so no one can look at them. You made up your own mind what people would say about them, and then you just accepted that judgment, without even testing it."

No, I want to say. *I got that judgment all right—from my mother, the kids, the teachers, my father, Steve, Cindy...even Mr. Wallace and that stupid lemon.*

But he doesn't pause to let me answer. "And when you're out there with those people, don't expect me to believe you show them yourself. I've seen you, remember? I know better. You put on a show for them, based on what they expect of you." His voice loses its harshness. "Why me? Why did you draw that for me, and not for anyone else? What's the big deal about my reflecting other people, wanting to please them, giving them what they want? Everybody does it! You give them what they want in unimportant things so you can do what you want in the things that matter."

I remember telling my parents I'd make good grades, even promising I'd go to college, if they'd just send me to Whitman (*just let me meet Graeme*). He's right, isn't he? That was the same thing. I was satisfying their expectations in order to do what mattered to me.

"What matters to you, then?" I ask him.

He stares at me and opens his mouth to answer, then closes it again. Finally he whispers, "My writing—writing things that mean something to my readers—writing..." And his voice trails off.

I shake my head, thinking of the second novel he's not writing and suspecting that's what he's thinking, also. I try to explain, "Everybody doesn't do it—at least not to the same extent you do." Coming here was so important I was willing to lie to my parents in order to let them think they were getting the son they expected. But I never intended to actually *be* that person. I was always determined to stay myself.

I think of Adrian's charm and Rachel's coolness, and pick my way deeper into understanding. "There's something behind the reflection, some part of them that makes them unique—if they try to please other people by giving them what they want, they're trying to protect what makes them special. They're scared other people will try to change it, or take it away. They're scared of letting anyone get close enough to do that." *I'm scared of letting anyone get close enough to do that.* "You do it

151

because it's the only thing you know. Maybe they're all worth far less than you are"—*I can admit that much*—"but they've got an inner self they'll do anything to keep safe. They're alive in some way you've never even imagined."

"I'm alive." His voice is almost a whisper. "I've got an inner self that makes me unique. Why didn't you draw what's inside the reflection?"

Did I get it wrong? "What is inside, Graeme?" That's what I draw—that's what I see in people. If it was too well hidden, then I failed. *I hope I did fail.*

"How can I answer that?" he asks, his voice almost angry again.

You can't, because there is no answer. I didn't fail—it wasn't there to see.

I try asking, "Why do you think we're here?"

He stares at me as if I've lost my mind. Maybe I have. "To make art," he says.

I nod. So he's sure of that much, at least. "That's why we're here at Whitman. I think"—I hesitate—I've never said this to anyone before—"that's why people are here on earth at all. I mean—lizards and cats and trout don't make art. Why do we do it?"

"Why?" he repeats, shrugging. "To show people what they're like—what society is like."

"No!" I shake my head, hard. "That's just the start. That's what I do with those sketches." I gesture loosely to the crumpled sketch on the gravel, but neither of us looks at it. "But that's not what art is really about."

He studies me, frowning. "What do you think it's about, then?"

"Art's about showing people what's possible," I say. I've never tried to put it into words, but that's what I do.

He considers this. "But—is showing somebody what's possible the only way to reach them?"

I shake my head, confused. "What do you mean?"

"In my books, I show people what they're doing and who they are so they'll stop and think about themselves."

"But do any of them think about that?" I demand. "Do they see what they could do to change themselves, or just what's gone wrong?"

He jerks back slightly, as though I slapped him. "I can't tell them what they ought to do."

No, you can't. I feel the dull ache of regret replacing the anger and betrayal I'd felt before. *I so wanted you to be able to tell me.* "But that's what art should do—offer some hope. Show how things *could* be."

Graeme looks at me steadily. "Is that what your paintings are about?"

I start to say yes— But then I stop. My paintings don't always show how things could be. I haven't really escaped the wolf pack yet, have I? I'm still running from them, hiding from them. And he can't show me how to stop because he doesn't know.

"Well, is it?" he prods.

"I try to make my paintings show what could be." I force myself to be honest. "But sometimes the best I can manage is showing how hard it is to strive, let alone achieve."

"Showing who?"

I blink at him, uncomprehending. "What do you mean?"

"Who do you show? What good does it do to protect something no one ever sees?"

I stare at him.

"What do your paintings matter if no one sees a single canvas, Charles?" His voice is stronger now. "Are you going to slash them all to pieces before you die? Or torch them? What good is pouring all this effort into protecting your paintings if they die with you, unseen?"

The fragments of colored glass in the kaleidoscope have shattered their case, silver-tipped shards of mirror flying at me.

"You talk about being alive or dead inside—you might just as well never have lived at all if everything you've created dies when you die. At least my book will survive, and people have read it, and maybe the book made some of them stop and think." Graeme pauses. "It reached you."

"It did," I whisper. "I only came to Whitman because I wanted to meet you—meet the person who was brave enough to expose the game."

The silence grows as I stare, unseeing, at the jagged gravel.

"Charles."

Has he beaten me at last? Or have I won? What was there to win, and when did we declare war?

"Let me see your paintings."

No more than that. I know I can refuse. But no one has come right out and just asked to see them. And I hurt him with my drawing (*with the truth*). I owe it to him to find a way to undo the hurt.

154

I stand up stiffly, brushing loose gravel from my jeans, and he rises smoothly without uncrossing his legs, with that dancer's grace again. I have no words to say as I lead the way down the stone stairs to the fourth floor, unlock the door, and stand aside to let him enter.

Excerpts from
Graeme Brandt's Journal

October 10 (Senior Year)

I didn't really expect Charles to let me into his studio. We'd hurt each other, brutally, even without wanting to, and I couldn't begin to guess at what he was thinking any longer. But I had to ask—and he let me in.

Nothing special about the room, except the little dogleg jut in the wall that crippled the neat rectangular shape. It was a studio, like all the others at Whitman, but I didn't see the room itself at first. All I could see was his work.

The room was filled with canvases. They were leaning against the walls, propped up on easels, hanging clear to the ceiling, none of them in any particular order I could see. I felt like I'd left the real world behind and entered a *Star Trek* holodeck. This was a magical universe overflowing with color and structure and emotion. Some of the paintings were so real I felt I could step into them and become—I don't know, more real than I was now. It wasn't always an inviting world they showed, but I could feel the truth. He had one he must have painted since he came here—the trees filled with birds that haunt the shortcut to the dorms. A figure strode through the trees, unfrightened, and for a moment it was me there, knowing where I meant to go, not caring about the screaming birds overhead. Then I knew it wasn't me at all. But it might have been.

Others were abstract, like a starry night van Gogh never dreamed of, with devouring skyscrapers closing in on the sky. The abstracts teemed with dizzying feelings, which Charles keeps bottled up and only releases in his paintings. There weren't any cute greeting card pictures, or adolescent explosions. He's a year younger than me, but his painting is all grown up. It's not some profound intellectual thing that doesn't make sense to anybody other than the creator, either. That was the strangest thing. It so clearly had a purpose: to communicate. Here, with only him to see them—it's as if they're incomplete, diminished without their intended audience.

What must it do to him to keep all of this locked away? Charles put all of himself into them, and then left them hanging on hold without anyone to see them and understand them. He's left himself hanging on hold, too. Why? It's got to hurt worse than having nothing to write, to have all this to paint, and not allow it to be seen.

I looked at the paintings for a long time. Charles never spoke, never stopped me from moving one painting to see what hid behind it. And there were paintings that showed me more than he might have wanted. Some were hopeless, or tried to be—a wolf pack closing in on a lone figure. A landscape of gray tree trunks like prison bars, a single wing straining outward between them, choking darkness behind the trees, and a loose scattering of white feathers on the shadowy ground below. A phoenix torn to pieces by lions, yet rising, reborn, above them. Like the phoenix, Charles kept on painting instead of giving up. He must have had the faith that someday someone would see them, and would understand.

Some were a dizzying blend of the real world and an abstract imagination—I suspect these are his masterpieces. In these he took reality and made it into possibilities that only he could imagine. That kind of dramatic transformation was what artists used to do, like Michelangelo sculpting a David who was at once vulnerable and beautiful and supremely powerful—a transformation of man into what he should be and could become. But today sculptors transform scrap metal into junk piles and call it art. Artists use computers to generate graphics that are supposed to be true to the real world. I write a book that shows us what we are, not what we could be.... And Charles Weston's paintings hang locked in his studio, protected from the world that needs to see them. Why did he come to Whitman to meet me? What did he think I could show him that he doesn't already know?

I turned from the blaze of color and feeling to the artist. Charles stood watching me, leaning against the empty wall of the narrow entranceway the jutting dogleg formed. In some ways, I saw him as I'd always seen him—attractive, with beautiful eyes that glitter and flicker and say things he won't put into words. But the protective mask that distorted his appearance in public was gone now. He'd left all his guarded uncertainty outside his studio. He was just waiting, at peace with himself. Right then he seemed more real to me than he ever had before, and I suddenly understood—this was what he had expected to see when he looked at me, because he'd thought my work was the same sort of warning as his wolf pack, or his single wing straining to escape the imprisoning trees.

That was when I saw just how great the difference between us was, and what he had been trying to explain to me on the roof. I'm not like Charles. I can't equal his creative integrity. I can't see the possibilities that he sees, and offer them to my readers as hope for the future. I can't even find a way to reflect it back to him. I can only write what is, and I've done that. I felt ashamed, because I knew I'd let him down, because I couldn't measure up to him.

I turned away—and then I saw it. If I'd seen it in a museum, in a textbook, I'd have figured the artist was a genius who'd outlive all the rest of us, not a teenage classmate I'd hoped to seduce. He had captured me, instead, and rather than offering me his body, he was offering me his hope.

I saw a canvas that showed a city under a sunset of swirling, electric, manmade fluorescent colors—vibrant pinks and shimmering reds—the lights from the sky intensified by the neon spots of city streets. The weight of dark clouds, heavy with night, pressed the charged brilliance down to earth. But up out of the neon haze rose a bell tower, sharply etched against the lights. As the clouds pressed down, dimming the fluorescent gleam, the manmade tower stood forth with increasing power, not giving in to the forces of darkness and nature. This is the human will that Charles believes in and can express more powerfully with his vision than anything I can express with my words.

As I looked at it, the cityscape worked its magic on me. I began to believe I could be something more, after all. If I couldn't remake the world the way Charles could, perhaps it wasn't beyond my gift for words and reflection to transform my image of that world.

And then I realized what I was going to write, the idea I'd been straining to find inside myself but couldn't bring into focus. Now that I've shown the world as it really is, and made Alan a reflection of the people around him, I needed to find a way to transform him—or, if not him, his brother, Kyle. I wasn't sure how yet, but Kyle was going to find a way to rise up, like that bell tower, to break away from the mirror he'd seen Alan become—the same mirror I'd let grow within me and around me. If I could write that, even if I couldn't change my real world, I could at least see some hope for myself, and maybe show my reader what he could become.

I looked back at Charles and smiled with the pride he'd always expected to find in me. I'd never truly felt it in myself until that moment. We stood, balanced, two creators, and finally I saw myself as he had always seen me.

And then I saw the caricature of himself that he had once told me about, with the hidden face. It showed him masked and disguised, a desperate, serious, fantastic Harlequin. He was armed with his pen and shielded with his sketch pad, and he stood guard in front of an easel that would betray his vision if he ever relaxed and let the canvas it held be seen. The drawing was right by his studio door, a constant reminder of the role he'd chosen to play in the world.

I reached into my pocket and felt the sharp edges of the crumpled sketch he'd made of me, the sketch I was going to remake as I remade myself. My mind was already shaping the book—the novel that Charles had pushed me toward and that Mr. Adler had been waiting for, and, most important, that I'd been aching for while empty thoughts chased themselves across the computer screen. Now he'd given me the purpose I'd lacked.

Holding myself erect, still gripping the pride and hope he'd given me to fill the emptiness I'd struggled with for so long, I faced Charles as an equal. "Thank you."

He said nothing, but the shadow of a smile flickered across his face.

"I understand that this"—I gestured to the painted world around me—"is your business. I won't say anything about it to anyone."

He didn't react, and I knew he didn't want to talk about it. How could I ever do anything for him that would measure up to what he had given me?

I started for the door and he moved aside to let me pass, but I stopped in that little entranceway. I had to put it into words, to be sure he understood. "Charles—I love you, for what you showed me here. Thank you."

We were close enough to touch, and he didn't draw back from me, but he didn't lean forward, either. If he had— But I didn't press him. Instead, I reached for the door and let myself out, leaving him in his sanctuary. By the time the door closed, my mind was fully on the book, on Kyle—becoming Kyle. He was to be myself, and he would fight my battle to break away from the roles and mirrors his family had accepted—had welcomed.

I didn't see the Whitman stairwell—I saw a crowded middle school hallway in Los Angeles. I didn't smell the paint and turpentine in the air—I smelled vinyl book bags and heard the slam of steel lockers that I remembered from my old public school. I felt the jostling of bodies in between classes, heard the principal's announcements, heard the kids talking back to the intercom. I could see the first chapter as if it had already come off my printer.

I hadn't felt like this since I was a kid making up stories in third grade. I felt I was truly an author. Somehow I'd finally become a creator, for real.

And then I knew how to thank Charles. I'd dedicate this book to him, and he'd see how he had changed me.

10

"What happened to the sketch of Graeme Brandt?"

Rachel's tone is even, not demanding anything, but I can hear she feels I've let her down. She saw me drawing him, after all. But I can't put that image of him in print. I couldn't, even before he looked at me on the roof, and asked to see my paintings. I certainly can't do it now, remembering him standing in my studio. It's a true sketch—it *was* true, when I drew it—but I don't know if it's still true. Something happened that morning, to both of us. Graeme Brandt may have changed. I may have changed. I'm not sure exactly how to draw him any longer. I don't try to explain that to Rachel, though. All I say is, "It didn't work out. Will the others do?"

"Of course." She shuffles through them and smiles. "I really like the one of Marc Worley."

He's in the drama department, and I drew him poised above a puppet theater, moving strings with every finger, a look of utter panic on his face in spite of the order onstage. "He's a nice guy," I say, looking out the window crammed between her office file cabinets as a flock of birds heads purposefully for the trees. "But he's going to have a heart attack before he gets to college if he doesn't take it easy."

She nods. "Too true."

I've given her two girls and three more boys to go with the drawing I did of Tyler originally, and I have no doubts about the truth in any of them. That will have to do.

"I don't know if you're interested," she says slowly. "You may not want to sketch him after all. But you've got some time to think it over. I'm planning to do a separate piece on Graeme Brandt in the spring. Would it bother you to sketch him then?"

I drag my attention back inside the cramped office. "Why would it bother me?" *What did you really see that night at the cast party?*

"The way you look inside people..." She's keeping her eyes on the sketches spread out on her desk, not looking directly at me for once. "I don't know what's inside Graeme Brandt, even though I've edited his essays. He's like a puzzle that doesn't fit together, that's missing a piece, maybe? Or a plastic puzzle where one of the pieces got too near a fire and warped. I thought maybe you'd see inside him and find a way to explain him."

You wanted me to dissect him and serve him up to you, didn't you? But why?

"But I only caught a glimpse of your sketch the other night, and it didn't make any sense—just pieces again." She raises her head and looks directly at me. "*Did* you understand him?"

I shrug. *You've got a crush on him, don't you, Rachel?*

Well, I hate to break it to you, but you're hardly his type... Or do you just have a thing for puzzles you can't solve? "Why the spring?" I stall. I tried to call Graeme the other night, to make sure he was okay, but there wasn't any answer in his dorm room, and I couldn't quite muster the nerve to knock on his studio door. I wanted to hold on to the way he looked when he saw my paintings. I want to believe he hasn't pulled away from me after seeing them. I want to believe him when he said—

"He's working on a new book," Rachel says. "I'm guessing he wants to finish it before graduation."

Hope suddenly leaps in my chest. Graeme hadn't known what to write before—now he's already at work on a new novel? Because he saw my paintings?

"If it's as good as *Eye of the Storm,*" she goes on, "he could graduate with a second contract." She smiles briefly. "Think about it—two published books before he even gets to college."

"When did he start this book?" *What did he see in my studio?*

She must hear something (*hope? happiness? fear?*) in my tone. She cocks her head to one side and studies me. "Charles, are you okay?"

I can't let her (*anyone*) guess that Graeme saw my paintings and they— What? Inspired him? *Not yet— not until I'm sure. And then I can let them all in, can't I? What I used to dream—at last. He really will be able to show me how to do it, after all.* But I have to be sure. I have to wait until I see what he writes (*until I see him again*). I make my neck relax enough to nod, and manage a grin. "Sure. I'm just tired. I've been painting a lot." *Liar. You haven't touched a paintbrush since Graeme left your studio, afraid of what you did to him—what the two of you did to each other. Except for stupid still-life blocks and cow landscapes. But now he's writing. Now you can paint again, too.*

"Well," she says slowly, her eyes unconvinced, "I thought I'd interview him in the spring, when the book's done. I hear he's like a hermit when he's writing his first draft, so there probably won't be a chance to do a piece on him until he finishes. I suppose he's planning on going out with a flourish."

Like a hermit—that's why I couldn't reach him. I try to squelch the stab of regret. *You thought, if someone* (Graeme) *liked your paintings—liked you—you wouldn't be alone anymore. You thought you'd have a friend with whom you could share the crippled tree, not find yourself still on the outside, this time stranded there by a hermit.* But that's okay—if he's writing, Graeme must be all right. If he's found a new book inside himself, then my paintings must have mattered more to him than my sketch. Maybe he'll even forget the things I said to him on the roof—maybe he'll prove (*to whom? himself, or me?*) that they're not true after all. And I can wait—wait until he's finished with the book, until he's ready to stop being a hermit, until he's ready to tell me he's forgiven me for the sketch because of my paintings (*or until he shows me he can't forgive the mirrors, ever*).

"Are you still there, Charles?"

Rachel is looking at me curiously, and I realize a hint of my being pulled between two possibilities shows on my face. I can't help it—I loved seeing him in my studio. I want him to forgive me. *I want him to be my friend.* I wonder how Rachel would look in my studio. What would her clear brown eyes see in my world of canvas and paint? For a moment I imagine her turning to me, her eyes alive, her face smiling, but that's a future hope (*a painting*) not a present truth (*a sketch*). It's too soon to believe it might really be possible. I ignore the ache in my chest at the sight of one strand of shining hair caught across her cheek and shrug. "Sure, I'm here. Whitman's going to have to make a new admissions videotape advertising Graeme's success to wow prospective students."

It's a pretty good answer, but she sits there, strangely still, studying me, and I can't see what she's thinking. *She's working out how to revise you, how to rearrange the pieces to show the potential she thinks she'll find in you.* I shift on the hard chair, wishing I could speed up time. How long does it take to write a book? How long do I have to wait?

"What would you like to draw for me next?" she asks. Perhaps she's accepted my reaction, or maybe she's kind enough not to push. Or maybe she's filed it away to fiddle with later, like sliding around the wooden pieces of her puzzles. I don't know which.

"Nothing," I tell her, realizing it's going to be hard to wait, now that I've started hoping. All I can do is bury myself in paint (*and hope he writes fast*). "I'm doing too much right now—I need some time to get caught up or I'm going to flunk Introductory Programming." Am I? That's the first course I can dredge up, but I haven't a clue how I'm doing in it. No, wait, Alona showed me part of the *Lord Jim* video game in class this morning, and it actually ran—the climax of the book as Conrad wrote it, but with the player making up Jim's mind for him.

"Will you fight?" she cried. "There is nothing to fight for," he said; "nothing is lost." Saying this he made a step towards her. "Will you fly?" she cried again. "There is no escape," he said, stopping short.

How do you answer her? Do you:

◉ a. Fight Doramin

◉ b. Fly from Dain Waris's death

◉ c. Finish the pretense by dying

She showed me how to program these graphic designs for the options, and I had to admit, my father was right to see possibilities in computer graphics. Alona even set up a point value for the choices so they add up to a final score at the end of the game. Not that scoring a lot of points means you've won anything, of course.

"Charles—"

"Sorry. Maybe next semester, okay?" Will he have finished the book in the spring, like she expects? Will I find out then that he's forgiven me, or will I have to face the fact that I'm destined to always be the outcast—seeing too much and hurting people with the truth? Oddly, it was easier when believing that someone might see my paintings and understand was only a distant dream, before I came to Whitman, when I only imagined that

Graeme Brandt could show me how to make the dream a reality. Now that it might actually happen—that I can dare to hope I'm on the verge of letting the people I care about see my paintings at last (*or on the verge of having it all come crashing down on me*), I'm afraid to count on it, afraid of failing. I'll paint a figure poised on the parapet of the studio roof—will he leap up, to soar free at last, or crash to earth forever?

I want to tell Rachel (*Graeme, someone*) all this, but I don't dare. Somehow I'm out of her office, out of the student center, into a sweltering afternoon, burning from the confusion of hope and fear inside me. Students crowd the sidewalks, heading for studios and practice rooms, and I want to grab them and say, *Look at my paintings!* But I can't—not yet—not until Graeme has written his book and I know, for sure, what we did to each other.

Then I'm up the echoing stairs and around the corner to my studio. My key grates in the hasp lock. Inside I just sit on the tile floor, my back against the smooth wood of the door, not seeing what is, but what was. Seeing Graeme looking at the cityscape. His face was beautiful, almost transformed. That's what I dared to hope for when I imagined people seeing my paintings, a transforming rapture. I itch to paint the figure straining toward hope on the parapet, but I'm too keyed up.

I go back to the dorm. Adrian's in his practice room, though he's left pieces of himself scattered across his half of the room. I see his CDs of Ravel, and Tyler's panic when I bluffed about the quartet flashes through my mind. Why did I stand up for Adrian? Why did I show Graeme himself?

I see the sketch I made of Adrian, still hanging there, and know the answer. Both were truths. Standing up for Adrian was right, because his quartet was true, it was his self transformed into music that spoke to all of us—even Tyler. That's why Tyler hated it. The sketch I made of Adrian shows that truth. The sketch I made of Graeme showed his truth, as well. But now Graeme is writing. Can the truth change?

I think of Graeme looking at my paintings, awed and excited. I could actually see something click into place in his mind as he stood in front of my cityscape, as if he'd found his way out of a maze. That must have been when the new book came into focus for him. He was more than the mirror then, wasn't he? Could I sketch him like that, a peace offering to undo the shock of that first sketch? I imagine going to his studio (*not knocking on the door, not going inside to him, not*—) and slipping the sketch under the door, envisioning his face as he unfolds it and sees—what? I pull out my sketch pad and uncap my pen. Lines uncoil on the page, straining to capture pride and the moment of inspiration as his tall form rises from a framed vision the viewer can't see. Instead of drawing his head as a mirror, it's a book, open to the first page, the first line just beginning to appear, the rest of the pages blank with the potential to become—anything. *Why can't I draw his face?*

It's not right, somehow. *The perspective is wrong…* But I shake my head, knowing it's more than perspective.

It doesn't have the ring of truth that reverberates in my sketch of Adrian, and I don't know why. If I could only speak to him, know he's all right, know what he's writing. He said he loved what he saw in my paintings (*loved me*), and I long to draw that love. But the sketch isn't working.

I pick up the phone. *Graeme is like a hermit when he's writing*... I punch in my parents' number, but of course they're at work. I leave a message on their machine. Why did I call? Perhaps just to hear my mother's recorded voice. To remind me of—what?

My copy of *Lord Jim* lies on my bed. It's not Introductory Programming I'm in danger of flunking, it's English. I think I have a paper due on the book at the end of the month. I wonder what day it is. I wonder if the English teacher would accept the computer program instead of a paper?

I've already read the book, but I don't know what to write. It's a frightening book—spare, rhythmic words that lull the reader the way the sea lulls its passengers. But dangers wait in the sea, and in the pages—reflected images rippling in the waves. Jim self-destructs because of the image he's created of himself. He can't live up to it, but he can't betray it, either. I wonder if I can turn in a paper proving that Robinson Crusoe's desert island (*with no Friday—no one playing Simon Says at all*) is preferable to Jim's admiring paradise of deadly expectations.

Which is true—the endless images, or the (*lonely*) self within? Which will Graeme choose, in the end? Or— the thought unsettles me—do we choose who we are, or are we born that way? If Graeme was born a mirror, *can* he choose to change? Or did he choose to become a mirror somewhere along the way, and can he revise that choice? Did he already revise it, as he stood in my studio? Is that why the new sketch isn't working, because I don't know what he chose?

I toss *Lord Jim* aside and get up, pacing to the window. How can I make it through this semester, until he finishes the book, poised on the edge, not knowing whether he'll join the wolf pack or be my way out? I tell myself to concentrate on nothing but the steps along the way—write the paper about Jim's failure, paint still lifes for Mr. Wallace, paint landscapes (*not cityscapes*) for Ms. Katz, paint portraits (*not Graeme*) for Mr. Thornton. Survive until spring.

But I can't focus on meaningless schoolwork. I want to hope that spring brings Graeme out of his writing seclusion transformed—the phoenix risen from the ashes. I'll know as soon as I see him. I'll know, the way I knew the truth at the party, on the roof (*in my studio*). I'll know whether I can let them all (*Rachel, Adrian, Alona, everyone*) into my studio, or whether I have to give up the dream forever.

Graeme Brandt's Journal

November 27 (Senior Year)

Finally back at school, and it wasn't the day I'd hoped for—it was better.

I thought Thanksgiving would never end. Family I hardly ever saw as a kid, and never see except at holidays anymore, and all those huge bowls and platters overflowing with food, and Kyle waiting while I tried to be polite to everybody but kept wanting to escape. Then I'd try to slip away, and they'd catch me staring out the window or sitting in my room, scribbling notes, and tell me it was supposed to be a holiday—well, Dad said that, and Aunt Theresa wanted me to tell everyone the story I was working on, and Uncle Kurt just rolled his eyes. Mom told them all to leave me alone—I was "writing." She must have told them to be quiet so as not to distract me—they were all practically tiptoeing along the hallway whenever they came upstairs.

Aunt Theresa tiptoeing is something like an earthquake... and I wanted to forget about Kyle and Whitman and Charles's paintings and go out in the hall and hug her. She thought my stories were so cute when I was little. I used to love to make up a new one to tell her, and she'd listen as if it was even better than her "stories" on television—she's so serious about her stories, she's even got the soap opera updates as the first number on her telephone's automatic dialer. She wouldn't care what Kyle did—she'd just listen, wide-eyed and nodding, and sigh at the end. I almost shoved the notebook under my mattress and went out to her. But I couldn't.

This book—I know what I want to write, I know what I want to have happen. I want Kyle to stop reflecting what other people want and to become someone better than them—better than they can even imagine. But it's not happening that way. Kyle won't do what I want him to. When I wanted him to face down the metal shop teacher, he wouldn't. He ducked out when he heard him coming into the shop room so that the other guys got caught, but after class he wired the welder so that it arced when the teacher touched it the next day. It didn't burn him, but it was a nasty shock—and it frightened him.

That wasn't what I meant for Kyle to do at all. I didn't want him to be—well, to put it bluntly, sneaky. Or mean. I don't know, maybe he's not really mean. Maybe he has to start out sneaky before he can get brave enough to stand up for himself. Or maybe I've got it all wrong. I only know I can't tell Aunt Theresa about Kyle. And I can't tell my parents this new book isn't working. I've got to make it work. I *will* make it work.

I dumped my stuff in my dorm room before anybody noticed I was back, and left a note for Mr. Adler that I was going to be in my studio working on the book. But I didn't want to read through Kyle's pages so far. I wanted to work out how he was going to change. So I just grabbed a reporter's notebook that would fit in my back pocket and took off. I wanted to think. I wanted—

Admit it. I wanted to ask Charles how he does it. How

does he paint like that? How did he find that bell tower inside himself and realize it in paint? If I could understand how he did it, I think I could see how I could do it with Kyle.

I was really hoping I'd run into him. Somehow, I thought he might come back early after the holiday himself. There were a few kids around, but they weren't Charles, and I didn't pay any attention to them. I was thinking about Kyle. I can't just move him around in the plot, like a pawn in a chess game. Or even a knight. Or even the king. They all get moved by the player, no matter how high they rank. But Kyle's got to do it naturally, or the book won't work. Why won't he do it?

I was striding down a gravel path, and poking and prodding at Kyle, knowing there had to be a way inside him, a way to make him work, and watching for Charles (trying not to look like I was watching for anybody) and I heard a girl call my name. Except I didn't recognize it at first—the name. She called out "Graeme," but I didn't feel like Graeme right then—I didn't even feel like Kyle. I was striding for a start, really stretching my legs, and I don't do that often because most people can't keep up with me. I stroll. But I was striding under barren tree branches, like someone else, someone I couldn't place. Then she called me again, and I realized it was Rachel Holland, and she was calling *me*. Graeme. The writer who can't write. . . .

I wondered at first if I'd missed a deadline—but I'd turned in my essay to *Ventures* before I left for Thanksgiving. It was an opinion piece about whether writers of one culture should be allowed to write literature about a different culture. It was good—Mr. Adler gave me an A on the original paper. So I just smiled at her and waited to get an idea of what she wanted.

Rachel didn't smile back. She looked at me and frowned. She's got this strange way of staring right into your eyes, instead of glancing at you and then looking away, like most people do. "Are you okay?" she asked me. "You look thinner."

I felt—I don't know—warm inside. It was a nice thing to notice. "Maybe I'm growing again," I told her, and laughed, because I'm tall enough.

She smiled a little, but not with her eyes. They still looked concerned, and I felt the faintest shadow of the affection in Aunt Theresa's hugs. So I gave Rachel a better answer. "No—it's just, all that food at Thanksgiving, it's kind of a turnoff." I shrugged. "And I've been writing. I guess I just haven't been thinking about eating all that much."

Her eyes had relaxed by then, so I added, "Besides, you can't ever be too thin."

"Or too rich," she finished, and her eyes were definitely smiling. "So—that's what I wanted to ask you about. How's the book going? Will you really have it finished before you graduate? Another contract? Rich and famous? I'd like to do an interview with you about it for the graduation issue."

"That'd be great," I told her, suddenly feeling how wonderful it will be to have two books sold by the time I got to college. Not just something excellent to actually *do* when you're still a teenager, not just what my parents hoped for, not just something Mr. Adler expected, but a real achievement—something terrific—something as great as those paintings.

And then I knew what I was feeling earlier, before Rachel had named me. I was feeling like Charles's figure, striding under those trees.

She must have seen my face change. "You look as if

something just hit you," she told me. "I'd better let you get it down on paper before you lose it."

I think I waved, but I didn't see her go. And I didn't pull out my notebook, either. It wasn't something I needed to write down then and there or I'd lose. It was inside of me now, a part of me. I turned back toward my studio, striding again, but this time the pace wasn't accidental. I was deliberately striding like the figure in Charles's painting, not afraid of the rustling cloud of birds overhead.

I hadn't seen Charles, but it was all right. Even better, in fact. I didn't want to ask him to tell me how to do this. I wanted to show him *I* could do it, myself. I could do what he gave me credit for. I'd seen that painting again, in my mind, and it showed me how. Don't be afraid of striding forward— just do it—just let Kyle grow and the story will follow naturally. Just become the figure in the painting. I lengthened my stride still further. The birds couldn't stop me. I had to get back to the book. I'd write until I found a way to show Kyle it was all right to be himself, to break free. I could do it. I *would* do it.

PART TWO

===

SPRING

11

There's an unfamiliar envelope in my mail slot Saturday, taking precedence over the usual letter from home—impersonal typescript and no return address, but mailed to me, undeniably—sent through the campus post. While I ride back up in the dorm elevator, I methodically pry up the flap, in no particular hurry. I slide out the creased sheets and unfold them as I head into my room, wondering vaguely who's bothered to write to me. I have no real sense of curiosity—I feel I've been on hold so long that I can barely remember that first flush of hope....

March 12

Dear Charles,

By the time you read this, you're bound to have heard that I died from a heart attack. You see, that's what I wanted them all to think. I wanted to do something that none of them would ever know, ever even suspect. I wanted to do something that was all my own, for once, and I wanted you to know because you're the only one who would understand.

I'm going to kill myself as soon as I mail this.

Stunned, I stand rooted to the mottled tan carpet in my room and rifle numbly through the pages to the last one, heartsick with terror that I already know who wrote this letter—and there's his name at the bottom of the final page. Graeme.

Mouth dry, not sure what to do, I look helplessly around me. Am I expecting to see someone appear who can save Graeme (*me*)? Or someone sweeping in, accusing finger outstretched to mark me, blame me? No sound outside in the hallway—I didn't even see anyone downstairs.

I've got to tell somebody—

I've got to stop him—

Where is everybody? Not even any sign of Adrian. I glance over at his mess and see the Houston paper spread out on top of the scattering of CD cases on his desk. There's the glaring headline—front page: LOCAL STUDENT FOUND DEAD.

I sink back into my desk chair, the colors in the room smearing into blackness (*the way his eyes went black, turned into bottomless pools when he saw my sketch*). I want to scream at him to wait, to stop, but it's too late. He'll never hear me again. He's already done it. *No— not good enough—don't settle for a euphemism, be clear and unambiguous.* He's already killed himself.

The dorm is silent because everyone else knows—

they're already in mourning. I'm helpless to stop him, and I don't know how to mourn.

But what did he mean, wanting them all to *think* he died of a heart attack? *I wanted to do something that was all my own, for once...* I turn back to his letter— black ink on white paper—black on white, drained of life.

I plan to inject a lethal solution into a cut on my hand and toss the needle into the trash outside my studio door—there should be about fifteen minutes left before the janitor collects the trash from our building. I'll die in my studio, no one will ever find the evidence, and they'll all think a heart attack finished me.

Probably none of them paid enough attention to what actually happened in my book to remember how the teacher killed himself when he thought Alan was blackmailing him. And the best thing about it was that the solution was untraceable in the bloodstream. No one's going to have a clue. Not even Mr. Adler knew that I tested the suicide plan by actually ordering everything I needed for it, to prove to myself that the teacher would be able to do it in the story. In a way, it's funny.

And not so funny. You were right, of course. I've lived up to their images all my life. And now they'll twist my death to fit their image, too—a kid who pushed himself too hard—a kid who wasn't so great at sports because he had a heart murmur. You know, I really liked playing baseball once—I even wanted to be a professional ballplayer, but that was before I realized I wasn't supposed to be a jock. I was supposed to be a writer. So what if the condition's rarely fatal and I'm supposed to be taking my medication if I feel any chest pains? I took care to leave the medication in my dorm room, instead of taking it to my studio. They'll say I forgot. They'll re-create me as a sickly student with an obsession, who poured everything into his writing and finally expired after completing his last novel. Mr. Adler will remember our talking about burnout at that cast party, and the sales pitch will make a fortune for my publisher.

But that's not the way it is at all.

When I left your studio that day, I knew what I wanted to write. Nobody, not even you, figured it out, but the reason I waited so long to start the new book was that I couldn't find anything inside me to write. I'd said it all in Storm, and I was drifting. Not even my short stories were working anymore, and it scared the hell out of me. But when I saw your paintings, that cityscape, I realized what I was missing, what I'd always missed. You created a universe without any interference from the outside, or in spite of the pressures from the outside, I guess, and your vision of just how much an artist could create made me open my eyes at last. It was up to me to create myself.

That's what this book was supposed to do—to create Graeme Brandt. I even called it Breaking the Mirror. But something went wrong. The main character was Kyle Travis, Alan's kid brother, and he was supposed to escape from the expectations that Alan had used to save and ultimately trap his family. Reflecting other people's images was the way Alan survived and succeeded, but it was also my way, as you figured out. If I could show Kyle how to break out, then I could break free as well.

It's not that Kyle never made it. But when he tried to be himself, to choose what he wanted, the other kids (and even Alan) didn't want anything to do with him anymore—they treated him like he was some kind of alien. Worse, he got scared that the choices he was making weren't really his own choices, that he was just choosing what he thought he ought to, trying to be different without knowing why. I know, that probably sounds weird to you. But you'll read the book and understand then. Kyle had to get rid of the only person who knew what he was going through, and then make a choice that was a compromise. In the end, he had to accept a role that was closest to the person he wanted to be. It was the best I could do for him, and better than I could do for myself. But you'll understand that, too.

You see, I'd known for a long time there was something missing inside of me. That was why I couldn't write another book. I could have written the same story over and over, with different characters and different settings, but they'd all be the same basic book because that seemed to be all I knew, and I couldn't demean myself to repeat myself forever. I thought if I could only fill that emptiness inside of me, I'd discover something new that I could write. And when I saw your paintings, I knew exactly what I wanted to say. When I realized I couldn't make it work in my book, it frightened me. I was afraid *you were right—I was nothing more than a mirror in the end. I was empty inside.*

But then I realized that creating myself in the book wasn't the solution. That would be showing them all what I was doing—still just doing it for someone else to see. I decided to find a way that I could do it for myself alone. So I kept on writing the book, because Kyle had taken on a life of his own, even if it wasn't the life I wanted to give him. The book had taken on a life of its own, and I wanted to finish it. But I also began trying to come up with a way I could prove to myself that there was something inside of me, filling the emptiness, something beyond their expectations—something just for me, something only I would ever know about. And then I knew.

In order to get away from their expectations for good, I have to die. This way they lose me, you see? My parents, my teachers, Mr. Adler, my editor, the kids who think they're my friends. None of them will have any control over my death, so I'm setting myself free from their expectations, if only for one brief moment. But it's my moment, and no one will ever be able to take it away from me. It will fill the emptiness for all eternity.

The only thing that hurts is that I'd have loved to see what it might be like to live as myself, longer than just for that moment. I can't quite imagine it, any more than Kyle could. You were right, you know. I searched and searched, but I couldn't find the self I was protecting behind the surface games. I told myself, when I first came to Whitman, that the secret lay in giving in to people in the little things so that I could have my own way in the things that mattered. But now, when I ask myself what matters, I don't have an answer. I thought—it must be wanting something, knowing what you want. But I can't think what I want that someone else didn't tell me to want. And if there's nothing that matters, there's nothing worth going on living for, anyway.

Why did I let other people shape me for themselves? I can't explain it. I never questioned it, never even thought about any of it until you came along.

But, Charles—what about you? I know why you hide in your studio now. You've let other people shape you, as much as I have. You blame them for making you hide, don't you? You think you pull on that Harlequin mask in order to protect your vision. But it's not anyone else's fault that you accepted their judgments about you or about your paintings—that was your decision, your condemnation of yourself. Why, Charles? Why did you let them cripple you? It's not something they can do without your consent. I have to face the truth that I let them shape me, but you're no different—you let them shape you, too. You have to find a way out of that studio—you can do it. And if you stay locked inside, pretending that they're keeping you there against your will, you're lying to yourself and lying to your art.

Are you a coward, Charles? I'd hate to think so after seeing your paintings, but you're terrified to expose the most important thing in your life to other people's scrutiny. Maybe I have so much less to say than you do, but at least I have the courage to say it out loud, to publish it where they can read it. I'm sure there are lots of readers who don't like what I write, jerks like Tyler, or kids who just don't understand it—but what about the ones who get the point, like you did?

How can you dare keep your vision locked away from the world? I can bear to publish what I see, even though it means admitting just how limited my vision is. For you it would mean confessing your hope, and taking responsibility for showing the rest of us what to reach for. And you need those viewers as much as they need you. You need people to see your art to make your work complete. You need those people who'll understand, and who'll take something from your paintings—maybe the strength to go on, maybe the strength to find a way out.

The artist I saw in that studio is the person you were always meant to be. How long can you deny him?

Good-bye, Charles. I loved you, and you gave me more than love. You gave me a purpose and a gift of being that is so precious it can never be repaid. I wish I could have lived longer with it, but just being myself, even for that moment, will make my lifetime worthwhile. Without you, it would have been meaningless, and I would have known only that I sensed an unnamed emptiness, and left it forever unfilled.

Graeme

I put the trembling pieces of paper down on my desk beside the remains of the envelope. It's Saturday, March 14, two days since this letter was written. It can't be later than ten-thirty, because I got up a little after ten, pulled on an old pair of jeans and a T-shirt, went downstairs to get my mail, and came back to my room with the two envelopes. It couldn't have taken more than fifteen minutes to do all that. I started to open the letter I didn't recognize in the elevator and then read it after I got inside my room. I couldn't have spent more than five minutes, maybe ten, reading, so it can't be any later than ten-thirty. How can I fill the rest of the hopeless minutes stretching into the empty future?

I force myself to go back to Adrian's newspaper and read the account of Graeme Brandt's fatal heart attack, picking my way through the newsprint as though it were a foreign language. They found his body on Friday the thirteenth (*Is that what you hoped for?*). He'd actually died on the twelfth. Then I see the photograph smiling at me, that engaging, irresistible image. I drop the paper as if it burns my hands the way it burns my eyes.

Graeme Brandt was killed by a heart attack in his studio (*a studio I sat in one stormy night last September, a studio I fled from*) on March 12. *Graeme Brandt was killed by a lethal injection, which he gave himself after seeing my sketch (after seeing my paintings).* Graeme Brandt is dead. . . .

My hands clench. I waited for you all the way through winter to the spring. I painted photo-quality still lifes for Mr. Wallace and pastoral cows for Ms. Katz, and ended up with the best computer program in the class, thanks to Alona. I worked and I painted and I even sketched for Rachel. I tried to find a way to deal with her, to make peace with Adrian, to survive the Christmas break with my parents, and to explain the curfew violations to Mr. Pullton. I made myself go on, because you were writing—you were working, and I could hope that showing my paintings to you had made a difference, that when you finished writing (*and had forgiven me for the sketch—for the truth*) we might actually be friends, and you'd help me begin to open myself at last.

Oh—seeing my paintings made a difference to you, all right!

I stumble across the room to sit on my bed, burying my face in my hands, images lurching into my mind. I can almost see Graeme killing himself. He'd have been satisfied, even eager, that thrill of joy infusing his face, the way I remember seeing him in my studio, the way I tried to draw him in that failed sketch. I shake my head from side to side to obliterate the image, harder and faster. I can't think. I can't let myself think. Graeme could escape, but I can't, and I can't even dare to think about it or I'll have to give in to grief and fury. I can't let myself cry.

My head slows down until I can sit motionless, my hands over my eyes. Then I force my hands down to rest on my knees. I study the hands as though they belong to someone else. They're steady enough, but they're clenched so tightly that the blood has drained away. I force them to unclench until they lie open. *Simon says . . . sit still; look like everything's okay, and it will be.*

I'm not shaking anymore.

I look steadily at the room around me, mechanically noting the familiar setting. Adrian's closet door open, a pile of dirty laundry on the floor, hangers crooked;

my closet closed, everything in place behind my door. A tangle of white sheet and gold woven blanket on Adrian's bed, a puffy blue comforter wadded up at the foot, a CD case open on the wrinkled sheet with the liner notes spread out—Stravinsky, I think—headphones lying next to it, the wire dangling from his CD player on his desk. A newspaper spread out on the desk, with a picture of a dead boy—

Oh, God! I can't stop seeing Graeme's body on the floor of his studio!

I hear slow footsteps in the hall and my fists clench again. How am I supposed to go out of this room and face other kids? Teachers? How am I supposed to face Adrian when he comes back? I have to talk to people—*and they won't know what happened!* They'll think Graeme died of a heart attack—*they won't know that I—*

No—I can't think now. I won't let myself think. Maybe later, when I can see things more clearly, but it's too soon and my mind runs away with itself.

Graeme . . .

There are things to do today, things like writing the foreign policy paper for Government. I should finish that today, before I go to sleep tonight, before I wake up tomorrow. I should finish reading *Candide* before French class next Friday. I could do that today—should do that today. Plenty of things to do to fill the empty hours—but thinking isn't one of them.

But— What did he mean by calling me a coward? He couldn't dream of how much courage it took to hold on to hope, day after day, knowing the wolf pack has almost caught up, knowing how completely I've disappointed everyone's (*Mother's, Father's, Rachel's, Adrian's, Graeme's*) expectations—

Or am I too much of a coward to face the truth? Was he right about my blaming other people, letting them cripple me? Have I been playing Simon Says all along, and lying to myself that I was protecting my art?

I stand abruptly, willing my body not to shake, focusing on the room, depending on the verticals of the walls to hold me upright. I'll get out of here. I'll go to my studio. I shut my eyes, then snap them open again. Etched across my eyelids I can see the half-finished painting on its easel, the shadow on the edge of the parapet, waiting for my brush to set it free in angel flight or to send it crashing into hell. I know how to finish it now.

I can see my cityscape as it stands, propped up against the wall in my studio. I can see Graeme's face, transformed.

Graeme!

I've got to get out, with other kids, where I can force myself to bury my thoughts (*kill my hopes for good*). I grab the letter, wanting to crush it to pulp (*wanting to smooth the crumpled pages*) and cram it in my backpack beside the failed sketch I once hoped would be a peace offering. Maybe Graeme was right. Maybe we all play Simon Says, one way or another. Maybe it's time for me to give in to it and play along. *Simon says... behave yourself in public.* It sounds like good advice for once. I give myself orders. *Simon says... don't think. Simon says ... don't shake. Simon says ... don't admit the truth about Graeme Brandt's death* (even to yourself).

Graeme Brandt was killed by a heart attack after finishing his last book. But then the kaleidoscope possibilities swirl around his death—Graeme Brandt was killed ... by a heart attack ... by an injection ... no, by a heart attack ... by himself ... no! by a heart attack ... by Charles Weston ...

No! Simon says: by a heart attack.

12

I shouldn't be here. At first it was just going to be a memorial service at the interdenominational chapel on campus. Then they announced they were going to have the funeral service at a nearby church—only two blocks off campus. I see the spire every day, and it won't be meaningless architecture anymore—it's going to tower over me in perpetual accusation. The Brandt family wants to have him buried there—something about an inspiration to future Whitman students. So I thought I had to go. But I was wrong.

It's Houston-hot inside the church, already humid and sticky in March, and only fans turning, spinning kaleidoscope dust motes over the murky crowd. An organ plays the most dismal music I've heard outside of an old Boris Karloff movie. *"It's always better in the movies,"* Graeme had said.

The family is ushered into the front row. More people file in, and then a woman faints (Graeme's mother?). It must be the heat and the people and the tension—or maybe an overdeveloped sense of the dramatic. A man (his father?) just stands there, patting helplessly at her face and looking around, and then a younger stranger (did Graeme have a brother? a cousin?) brings her a glass of water and she sits up, sipping it and shuddering, and I envy her for being able to show how much she hurts—and for having people to comfort her.

Now the minister's voice rings in my ears, reading out the particulars—heart attack, plucked in the flower of his youth, unusually gifted boy, such great potential. They're the same words he'd use for a promising high school football player, probably almost the same thing he'd say for the local dogcatcher.

Then he looks directly at the crowd of students and family and strangers, his voice low and sincere so we have to lean in close to catch it. Graeme's mother holds a handkerchief to her mouth.

"I can't tell you that there's an earthly guarantee that he'll go to Heaven, but I believe that Jesus exists, and I know that Graeme will be with Him."

What's that supposed to mean? And now he reads something from the Bible—Revelations, I think. What does any of this have to do with Graeme? None of these people has any idea what revelation he had. None of them knows Graeme, my Graeme.

Now we're all standing, slapping pages softly in our hymnals to find Hymn 224. My voice won't hold steady; it quavers like it hasn't done since I was a little kid and felt shy of the high notes I could hit. My tenor betrays me now, splitting notes as though it's never sung out loud before.

Now the laborer's task is oe'r;
Now the battle day is past;
Now upon the farther shore
Lands the voyager at last.
Father, in thy gracious keeping
Leave we now thy servant sleeping.

It was some battle for you, Graeme. But what was it for? What did you win? What was your task in the end? My hands shake as I hold the hymnal, and I'm grateful to be hiding in the back of the church where I don't have to share it with anyone. *Simon says...control yourself.* I force my hands to be still and command my voice to hold steady.

There the tears of earth are dried;
There its hidden things are clear;
There the work of life is tried
By a juster judge than here.

How can they ever try his work, those angels and gods of faith or heart? And what makes these people who barely knew him think that God can know Graeme any better than they did? Dregs of long ago Sunday school lessons wash across my mind. If man was created in God's image, what was Graeme Brandt? Adam had the will to do other than what was blindly expected of him, Judas repented, and Peter denied. Even Jesus doubted and questioned and prayed for God to take away the cup of death. Man wasn't made in God's image to blindly copy anything or anyone around him! So how can God understand Graeme?

I slam the hymnal shut, ignoring the looks from strangers around me, and drop the book into its slot before I lose it totally. I'm not thinking straight.

People parade past the casket. From the back of the church I watch them, some reaching out to touch the folded hands with an intimacy none of them has earned. A couple of older ladies even have the nerve to kiss him on the forehead. These people have no right to use him this way. They never even knew him—how can they pretend his death means so much to them?

Mr. Adler stands over Graeme a minute or so longer than the others. Did he understand Graeme better? I remember Graeme's respectful kindness to him that night (*the night I drew the sketch that killed him*). Graeme recognized his mentor's claim on him—maybe Mr. Adler did understand his student, or at least did care for the person more than the celebrity. He looks into the dead face as though he's sanctifying a vow of some sort, and he stands straight in that crowd of hunched-over mourners.

The line limps forward until it's my turn. Graeme lies there, dressed in this stiff suit (*not an open-necked shirt that let me see the hollow of his throat as he looked at me in his studio that night, not tight jeans, not a shirt with the sleeves rolled up so you could see the long line of his arm, not even his hand turned so you could see the cut where he—*). I guess his parents saw him in a suit like that. Their famous author son.

The undertakers have put this fake smile on his face, nothing like the smile I remember. They blurred the details of death with makeup, and even darkened his hair from the soft black I knew. In front of all those ignorant strangers, I have to look at that dead waxy face and see, instead, the clear blue eyes of last fall, Graeme's eyes, in the sanctuary of my studio, measuring me in terms of my paintings, eyes that respected me (*too much*).

I want to reach down and shake him. *You're just playing another role! Stop it and get up*— But he can't get up, ever again, because he thought he could find himself in death.

I cut my thoughts off and twist my face away. I can't think about how wrong he was. Graeme Brandt is dead, and nothing can touch him now, nothing (*not even me*). I follow the procession out to the graveyard that encircles the church, and we wait on a fake plastic grass carpet that has been rolled out over the soft spring grass beside a deep hole ripped in the turf. The family sits on folding chairs up front, Graeme's mother sniffing into her handkerchief, his father staring uncertainly at the hole. There are still more flowers, their petals ruffling in the breeze (*as the breeze ruffled Graeme's hair on the roof that morning*).

Then the pallbearers carry out Graeme's coffin and rest it on glaring chrome rails set up over the grave. The minister smiles compassionately at all of us, and I look away, studying the drifting wisps of clouds in the pale blue sky above. It's as though some artist has taken a canvas of pure, flowing light and dragged his brush carelessly across it with feather strokes of shifting milky whiteness.

Someone from the row of family chairs weeps loud tears suddenly—an aunt? Did Graeme love her? Did he tell her secrets when he was little? She huddles, massive in a tweedy suit, a ridiculously small feathered hat pinned to her coiled black hair (*Graeme's hair*), rocking herself back and forth, choking her ragged sobs into her hands as if embarrassed to be caught sobbing out loud. I wish I could show my grief like that.

Then the minister clears his throat, and her sobbing eases. He stares out at all of us, holding his prayer book, and intones, "Man that is born of woman, hath but a short time to live, and is full of misery. He cometh up, and is cut down, like a flower; he fleeth as it were a shadow, and never continueth in one stay."

I stand rooted to the plastic grass, refusing to look at the coffin above its gaping hole, but the earth seems to lurch and everything tilts sideways through a sudden wash of tears until I can see nothing. *Graeme . . . he fleeth as it were a shadow, and never continueth in one stay.* But now, surely now he's reached home at last. Surely he achieved an end to other people's roles and expectations. He's dead, for God's sake! . . . *and never continueth in one stay . . .*

"In the midst of life we are in death; of whom may we seek for succor, but of thee, O Lord, who for our sins are justly displeased?

"Yet, O Lord God most holy, O Lord most mighty, O most merciful Saviour, deliver us not into the bitter pains of eternal death."

Death. *In the midst of life we are in death.* No, that's not the way it should be. It's not the way it has to be! I hear words, like a dull echo in the back of my head: "You're dead, Graeme—you're dead, inside, where you should be most alive, and you didn't know..." I can still see the shock on his face, flooding his eyes, turning them black in fear and emptiness.... *The bitter pains of eternal death...*

"Thou knowest, Lord, the secrets of our hearts; shut not thy merciful ears to our prayer; but spare us, Lord most holy, O God most mighty..."

I shake my head violently, to knock loose all possible thoughts. *Thou knowest, Lord, the secrets of our hearts, the secrets which we can't even admit to ourselves, the horrible, frightening, hurtful secrets that we don't dare confess...*

"Unto Almighty God we commend the soul of our brother departed, and we commit his body to the ground, earth to earth, ashes to ashes, dust to dust; in sure and certain hope of the Resurrection unto eternal life, through our Lord Jesus Christ."

Eternal life. Death. *You're dead, inside, where you should be most alive.* And his ultimate comeback. *I'm setting myself free from their expectations, even if only for one brief moment. But it is my moment, and no one will ever be able to take it away from me... Just being myself, even for a moment, will make a lifetime worthwhile...*

He fleeth as if it were a shadow, and never continueth in one stay...

You're dead, Graeme—you're dead, inside—you're dead—you're dead—and those eyes, black and lifeless in horror, staring back at me, believing me, accepting what I said. I passed judgment on him and sentenced him to death, and he carried out the sentence himself....

Thou knowest, Lord, the secrets of our hearts; shut not thy merciful ears to our prayer; but spare us, Lord most holy... I killed him. I told him he was dead, and he believed me. He never broke free, he never came to life—he killed himself because I told him that *I* saw him as dead already, and he believed me. First he tried to fill that emptiness by reflecting my expectation of him, and when he couldn't play the role of creator, he played the condemned role I'd written for him, not even realizing what he was doing. *Charles says... you're dead, Graeme...*

I killed Graeme Brandt....

Graeme Brandt was killed by a heart attack in his studio. Graeme Brandt was killed by a lethal injection, which stopped his heart and froze his lungs on a soft spring afternoon. Graeme Brandt was killed by Charles Weston, by a truth that never had to be spoken, a truth that killed Graeme's eyes and turned them black and empty—by a vision of paint he never should have been allowed to see....

Thou knowest, Lord, the secrets of our hearts.

They've lowered him into the ground and shut away the dead face forever. People are leaving. His mother is sobbing to the family. "Graeme was such a gifted writer. I always knew he would write great books, important books, even when he was just a little boy. He was such a good boy, so affectionate, so understanding—he always knew just what you wanted, and he was always there when you needed him, with just the right word or the right gesture..."

Man that is born of woman, hath but a short time to live, and is full of misery. He cometh up, and is cut down, like a flower; he fleeth as it were a shadow, and never continueth in one stay... Graeme never had a chance, not really, I try to tell myself. That woman, his mother—she wanted him to be the way he was. They all did.

But you killed him.

The pain inside me is growing past the point where I can take it, past the point where I can bear to stand here, surrounded by Graeme's people—

They were right after all, dressing him in that suit and smearing makeup all over him. He's still playing roles for them, as he played roles all his life, forever.... He was playing a role when he died, the role I assigned him. My role—my fault.

I murdered Graeme Brandt.

13

I haul myself up the stairs to my studio, feel the hasp lock shuddering in my right hand, concentrate on its solid weight as the unsteady key in my left hand skitters across smooth metal. Just get inside.... *Don't think, don't see Graeme, proud and tall when he left me that morning, proud as he must have been when he wrote me that letter—*

I jerk the lock free and slam the door behind me to block off the images. My studio...safe—

But the images crowd inside with me. I see Graeme, staring transfixed by my cityscape. I hear my voice, pronouncing his death sentence.

No! Not here—not my studio! This is the one place I can always be me, the one escape from what everybody else thinks, the one place I belong. Only this time I'm not trying to escape them. This time I'm trying to escape myself, and my studio is no protection against that.

I slam the door again, this time from the outside, banging the hasp lock shut, protecting my studio from the real danger, from the destroyer I've become. Where can I go now? Where can I hide? The dorm...but Adrian will be there. He'll know. He sees too much, with his composer's precision and his shrink's brain. The roof...but I recoil from climbing the stone steps, knowing I'll only see Graeme up there, his eyes black and dead—*the shadow poised on the parapet, crashing into hell...*

Down the stairs and outside. No one notices. The other kids, they've got their own griefs and fears, no pain wasted on mine. Got to remember, though, keep away from adults. They might see, and think they can help. No one can help. *Simon says... behave yourself in public. Be a good boy... Yes, Mother...* I want to call home, hear her voice, hear my father, but what could I tell them? What could they say? *Make everything all right, please*— But no one can. I've made everything all wrong.

How do you accept killing a friend? How do you accept a friend who allows you to kill him? How do you accept a friend who forces you into the worst Simon Says game of your life, who just gives himself over to you and lets you judge him, condemn him, and sentence him? *Charles says...*

I should never have come here to meet Graeme Brandt. I should have stayed in that stupid everyday high school, learned to hide myself from the wolf pack and to care, instead, which team kicked a ball in which direction, gone to a business school, gone into advertising, given up painting except in my locked studio— never reached out, thinking there was anyone else like me. I should have ignored Graeme after I saw what he was that first night, turned away from him when he tried to reach out, cut him off.

Cut them all off. Rachel—I have to stay away from her. I can't trust those analytical eyes that look inside me to take apart the pieces of myself. I can't let her revise me (*fix me—make everything all right*). Graeme wanted to look inside me and I killed him. Adrian—I have to destroy the drawing, stop him thinking we're friends. If he knew me, knew what I'd done to Graeme, he'd hate me as I hate myself. *But there has to be someone...* Stay with faceless, empty people (*like Graeme?*), people who expect me to be empty, too; people who won't look inside me, who won't pry behind the mask, who won't even care that the mask exists.

I walk, hands clenched in my pockets, past the concert hall with its music practice rooms (*Adrian*), down a twisting path that seems dimly familiar. My stomach heaves in sudden recognition and I turn, striding through soft grass, running away. My feet carried me to Graeme's studio... *Where I turned away from him... where he killed himself... where he carried out my sentence...*

My hands ache and finally I notice something warm and sticky on my palms. I pull my hands out of my pockets and stare dumbly at red-rimmed fingernails. I've ground them into my palms until the flesh is bleeding. I stand on the new spring grass with Graeme's studio behind me, watching the red smear oozing along the lines in my palms.

Good! I jam my hands back inside my pockets, savagely clenching and unclenching my fists, enjoying the punishment. But it's too small a payment for the crime of murder. I have to find something I can do, something gaping and ugly that I'll see for the rest of my life, some fair value payment to remind me that I killed Graeme Brandt. I drown in images of slashing my left hand, crippling my fingers so they'd never draw again the way he'll never write again, or blinding myself, blackening my own eyes as I blackened his, shutting out color on canvas forever.

But I couldn't do it. My shoes hit the pavement, the writers' studios far behind me now, and I follow a different path blindly. I can cripple myself so that I can just barely paint, but I'll always find some way to express my art, unless I take my own life. And I don't have that much courage (*that much cowardice?*). I don't even have someone who'll take the responsibility of handing me that death sentence. All I can do is destroy others, the ones who get too close to me, who don't measure up to what I think they should be. Viciously I grind my fingernails deeper into my palms.

"Charles!"

There is no one. I refuse to turn and look for a person who thinks she knows me, who wants to see inside of me. *A person I want to turn to.*

"Charles, wait! It's Rachel. Charles—are you all right?"

A hand clutches my arm and turns me. She looks into my face, her brows drawn together. Then her eyes widen. *Fine,* I think grimly. *Now you see—I'm an outcast, all right? I don't belong here. So just let me go.* But, perversely, her grip tightens.

"What's wrong?" she asks in an unsteady whisper. "I saw you—at the funeral." Oh, God. She was there? What did she see? "Your hands—" How did they get out of my pockets? She's staring at the blood on my palms. "What's happened?" She shakes her head. "Never mind. Look, the center's right over there. Come to the office and we'll clean you up."

Simon says... come inside and Mommy will clean up that scrape... If only it could be that easy.

I'm staring at her blankly, wondering why she stopped babbling. Was I supposed to say something? I don't have anything to say. I've never sketched her—I don't know her, not truly. Is she really apart from the games, or did I only want her to be? *Charles says... you're dead, Graeme... Charles says... you're like me, Rachel.* But what is she really like? Does she see too much, like Adrian? Does she really think she likes (*loves*) me? Maybe she does. Maybe we could have been friends, or even more. But that's false hope trying to rise from cold ashes. She wouldn't even want to know me, if she knew.... Why can't she just go away?

Instead her hand tightens on my arm, tugging firmly. "Come on." And my feet move, following her lead. I try to clean my mind, scrape off the paint and douse my canvas with turpentine, try to blot out my responsibility for Graeme's death, try to convince myself I should be grateful for someone's concern, and not rip her hand from my arm and shove her away before I contaminate her—or before I see into her and see truths I don't want to face.

Her sense of purpose drags me along beside her,

helpless, obedient, as though I'd been waiting to give myself over to her care and understanding. But I don't want her understanding. I don't want her to take me apart and reassemble me so the best pieces fit neatly and the others are discarded and the new Charles Weston she has created is forgiven. Even my studio can't protect me—how can Rachel's revisions fix me? She'll find some tidy way to delete the guilt, the pain, and bring out my potential in a polished new version of me. But that would be a cheat. I killed Graeme—that has to count for something! It has to be paid for.

"Come on inside."

One bronze door creaks open, the muses in the border frieze mocking me. *Adrian says . . . show time . . .* I follow her inside, through the front hall to the unreliable elevator. The door inches closed and the elevator groans upward. This would be a good time for the decrepit cables to snap at last. I'm ready now. A metal coffin (*like Graeme's*) plunging into the basement, burying me inside its crushed walls. That would be fair. Well, probably not to Rachel.

Somehow we're at the *Ventures* office, and it's deserted. "Between issues," she explains, unlocking the door. "And I wasn't the only one who wanted to go to the funeral."

Simon says . . . nod your head . . . say something. But the muscles refuse to work, and I stand there, caked blood drying on my hands, anger beating inside my head, pounding at my brain. *Get out of here—get out where you can be alone again, where you can find your punishment.* My left fist clenches suddenly, and I look down to see fresh blood seeping out of the palm. I see Graeme lying dead in his studio. *Blood pays for blood . . .* I squeeze my eyes shut, trying to blot out the image of blood cascading out of my left hand, no longer just gouges in my palm, but jagged slices across my wrist. I yearn for the blood.

"Here, give me your hands. Now it's going to sting, I'm afraid."

How did we get into Rachel's office? And was that satisfaction in her tone? I sit on the hard chair, and she's half propped against her desk, half bending down over me, her straight, soft hair falling forward like a veil. She's wearing a dark blue dress with a high neck, a small gold cross dangling from a chain around her throat. She was dressed for the funeral. I realize I'm still wearing the jacket and tie, not even noticing the choking tightness at my throat, welcoming it perhaps. She dabs my left palm with a damp cloth and it burns, and I welcome that, too, pressing my hand against hers through the cloth.

Maybe I was wrong. Maybe it wasn't satisfaction in her voice, maybe it was tenderness. After all, she doesn't just take her puzzles (*manuscripts, authors, paintings*) to pieces, she puts broken things back together, better than they were originally. But I can't be put back together and improved. Neither can Graeme.

She's looking at me strangely, holding my hand now, and looking deep into me, through the mask and into my mind's hidden den, where my consciousness hides and twists, trying to make itself small and innocent and hopeful again. But her eyes can see it. They tell me she was never deceived by the sketches I made—she knew what I was hiding in my studio. They tell me she knows all about me, she accepts me, I have to accept her, we are alike—

No! I thought Graeme and I were alike (*I wanted him to be like me, and he wanted to be whatever I wanted*), and I was a fool—a fool and then a murderer. I took more than Graeme's life—I killed everything he might have become. He never had a self before, but he didn't miss it. I decided he'd never have one at all. But what if I was wrong? I stole his hope. And he dragged the shreds of it together to make one last gesture, and it was nothing more than a sham, because of me!

I'm not like you! I want to scream at Rachel, and still her eyes bore into me, promising acceptance, offering— love? It's as though she sees my paintings in my eyes, and she wants to love me for what I do, what she thinks I am (*Does she want to be who I want her to be, too?*). But she doesn't know what I am—a murderer, a destroyer. The shaking inside my head is so great it must bring the student center crashing down around our heads, but nothing happens.

"Charles, you're trembling." Her voice is low. *Graeme's voice was low, an invitation to whatever I wanted, another storm—*

Rachel leans closer to me. She reaches out one hand to caress my cheek, gentle and cool as a clean brush filled with watercolor. Then her lips press against mine, and at their touch everything inside me is shaken to pieces. My mind shatters all the safety catches that keep my two worlds apart.

She has no right to study me, to think she could fix

what's wrong and love the improved me. I wanted to punish myself for what I did to Graeme (*for becoming the ultimate Simon to him*). Now I want to punish Rachel for what she's trying to do to me (*for becoming who I want her to be—but that's not what I want! If I made her think I needed her, though, I can make her leave me alone. I can make her hate me—I should have made Graeme hate me before he—*). My breathing is ragged, and the room turns black as if an entire ebony tube were smeared thickly across the canvas with a palette knife, and I leave rusty streaks of drying blood on the sleeves of her silky dress, gripping her arms as if I would crush her, and at the same time as if she were made of infinitely precious spun glass.

I'm out of the chair and pressing her back against the wall of file cabinets in the crowded office, crushing her mouth under mine, gripping her head between my throbbing hands, feeling the satin smoothness of her hair, then twisting my fingers in it. Now she'll know what I'm like, how I destroy things, and she'll stop trying to fit the pieces together. She'll stop wanting me. But— She should be pushing me away, as I tried to push her away before. Now that I've turned against her, she should be screaming at me. But the only sound is my pounding heart, and her hands aren't shoving me away, but reaching for me—why? Pulling me closer?

I push myself upright, away from her, my aching hands against the cool metal of the file cabinets, and look at her clear eyes, eyes still reaching into me, more confident now, compassionate—*controlling?* I recoil, shaking my head.

"Charles—"

My left hand, always truer, slides up the smooth metal to the top of the cabinet, gropes, my eyes never leaving her face. Then my fingers close around one of her puzzles, polished wood and pale cord. I grip it, the braided cord scraping my raw palms, and hurl the pieces to the floor.

"No!"

Finally I've spoken aloud.

"I don't want you to take me apart!"

I grope for another puzzle and shove it onto the floor as well. "You can't fix me and put me back together again! No one can."

Then I take hold of one of the kaleidoscopes.

"Don't!" she cries, tears in her voice. Now, too late, she's pushing me away.

I hold the tube with its core of shattered colors out of her reach. "You can't take everything apart and think you can make it all right again. Some things just can't be put back together!" *I can't. Graeme can't. Maybe Rachel can't.*

I loose my fingers and the tube rolls free, smashing into shards of glass on the floor. Then I turn my back on her and leave, willing the elevator to plummet me into oblivion at last, but it jerks its way down to the first floor in unforgiving safety. That's fair enough. Why should it offer me a way out?

Blindly, I walk again. I have to go to ground, somewhere. I'm shaking, and I don't know why. It's a spring afternoon, not winter any longer, and Houston wasn't even that cold in winter. But my teeth are chattering—

loud enough that I can hear them, like loose marbles rattling. With nowhere else to turn, I walk through the tunnel of trees. I see the green fuzz uncurling on their skeletal branches and know the birds will be back soon, if only this terrible cold goes away. And then I see my dorm past the last trees, and head for my room.

14

"What's wrong?"

I huddle, freezing, shivering with the cold. How can
it be so cold?

"Charles?" Footsteps shuffling on rough carpet, loud
scuff sounds scraping my eardrums, his whisper shouting in my head. *I'm sorry,* I want to tell him. *I didn't
mean any of it—I didn't want to hurt Rachel. I didn't
want to hurt anyone. Forgive me. I didn't mean it to
turn out like this. I never wanted to play!* But my teeth
are clenched so tightly against the cold that I can't
squeeze words through them.

I feel his hand on my blanketed shoulder. I tremble
at the touch, my face wedged between my pillow and
the wall. Are there second chances?

"God, you're freezing."

The hand is gone, just the scuffing sounds sand-
papering my ears. The voice is wrong. Do voices change
when you die?

"Here." A rush of air, and a muffling weight settles
over me. A quilted comforter, solid, thick, and no com-

fort at all. But the fingers on my left hand curl around it, clutching it through the cold. *Thank you. Does this mean you're not angry with me?*

A thud into the carpet, into my brain. No answer in words. Another thud. Then a sudden weight on the side of the mattress, a hand against my face, pushing the hair off my forehead, a warm, dry hand, a mother's hand. But she's far away. *Mother says...*

"You've got to calm down. You'll shake yourself into pieces like this."

But I'm already in pieces. I've got to shake myself together somehow.

The weight shifts on the bed. The comforter and the covers lift, and I wait for the icy blast that will shatter me for good. Instead, there's warmth. Pressing against me, huddling with me as the covers fall back into place. Not a chill tangle of sweat-soaked sheets, but a warmth like summer, pressing itself against my back, wrapping warm arms around my chest, warm breath on my neck. Living breath.

"No!" The word explodes out of me, as though the warmth has thawed the ice clenching my teeth. "I won't—" But even as I cry out, I don't want the arms to let me go (*even though it's not Rachel, never Rachel, not after—*).

"Shh. I know." *What do you know?* "It's all right. Just calm down and try to get warm."

And I lean back against the warmth. "Please—you've got to tell me—" I'm whimpering, but I can't help myself.

"What?"

I force the words through chattering teeth. "How to play the game (*at last*) and still find some way to stay me." I'm not making any sense.

"There is no game. And you're doing just fine at staying you."

"But how do you show your art (*yourself*) and not get torn apart, if you don't play the game?"

Time stretches and the bed shudders beneath me (*us*) as I try to stop shaking.

Finally: "You don't have to play any games, Charles— just do what feels right to you. You won't really get torn apart, even if it seems that's what's happening."

No—that can't be true. "But it's all Simon Says, every day. You do what people expect you to do, or you don't and they hate you for it."

"Simon Says?" I hear a faint chuckle. "Well, that's one way to explain life. But if you look at art that way, the artist is the one showing people what to do—artist Simon, in the center, creating options." *The mirror in the center . . .* "Then the viewer chooses to play along or not. See? Nothing to shake yourself to pieces over."

Do you—*who?*—mean that? Not Rachel, who decides how to assemble fragments. Not Graeme. But I still can't . . . Then I recognize the timbre of the voice, and feel the shape lying against me in the dark. Fully clothed, except for shoes. No threat. No demands. Not playing games. Not tearing me apart. Just holding the pieces together.

Not Graeme. Adrian.

"No—" I try to pull away from him. *Why didn't I destroy that drawing?*

214

"Don't worry," he says dryly. "I'm not going to do anything."

Not an invitation to a storm. I lie there, unspeaking, my eyes squeezed shut and my face damp beneath. He doesn't get up, doesn't move, just holds me. Uncounted minutes pass in the shivering, almost dreamlike darkness. You can say anything in a dream. "Aren't you afraid?" The words sound hollow, a shadow voice in the dark.

A pause. "Afraid of what?" His voice is soft, at once curious and impersonal. A safe voice.

"Afraid they'll hate you when they hear your music? When they realize who you are, and what you can do?"

Time stretches again, until, "Everybody's afraid of being rejected," he says slowly. "I want people to like my music—to get something out of it. But if they don't, they don't. Some of them may be nasty about it, but I don't think anyone really hates me."

I think of Tyler. *They do.* "Or is it because you're gay?" I press him. "Do you just expect them to hate you because you're different and don't bother to hide it by even pretending to play Simon Says? So it doesn't matter how extraordinary your music is?"

Unexpectedly, he laughs. "It's not exactly a trade-off, you know! Hate me for being gay, or hate me for writing music, but one way or the other, you'll end up hating me."

But it's not just any music, not even just good music—it's extraordinary music, and that's what they hate—doesn't he realize that?

He sighs. "If I didn't know better, I'd guess you were trying to insult me."

Am I? Am I pushing him away the way I pushed Rachel away? But I wanted Rachel, and I didn't trust her. I don't want Adrian, and yet he's here, and I don't want him to go. "I'm sorry," I whisper.

He doesn't draw back. "That's all right."

Then I ask, "If they hate you, can you change?"

"Well," he says slowly, his voice serious again, "some things you can't change. I can't change the fact I'm gay. I can't change the fact I compose music. But, other things—you change as you run up against life, as you see things about yourself you like or don't like. As you make decisions, or choices, you change. Not just because you think somebody doesn't like you." After a few moments of silence, he adds, "Believe it or not, I don't really expect everyone to hate me. Do you?"

The words are out before I think. "Of course I don't hate you!"

"Well, thank you for the backhanded compliment"—and I can hear the smile in his voice—"but I meant—do you expect people to hate you? Are you afraid to show your paintings because of that?"

If it weren't for the dream state around us, I couldn't answer. In the freezing dark, however, I breathe, "Yes."

He considers this. Finally he says, "I can't believe anyone could hate you for your art. Be jealous, maybe, but that just goes along with talent."

"No—not jealousy." He's got to know the truth. Maybe I am trying to push him away, like I did the others. "Everyone (*Mother, Father, Steve, Cindy, Graeme*) who sees my paintings turns on me. They—they hate me and want me to be someone different. (*Or they love*

216

me and kill themselves...) I'm afraid I'll change too much—become who they expect—lose myself."

"You don't have to lose yourself," he says quietly. "That's not the sort of change I meant. Choosing to change isn't the same thing as feeling pressured into changing into someone you're not." After a moment he adds, "It sounds as if you've shown your work to the wrong people. Or maybe you're being too hard on yourself."

"But you don't know what I've done," I whisper, cringing.

"Whatever it is, I don't hate you." He pauses. His voice is serious, not his light, teasing tone, and his arm around me is a promise. "You don't have to play Simon Says here."

Adrian pulls the comforter up to my neck, and his hand brushes mine. My stiff fingers, dried blood still rimming the nails, close around his. And I sleep.

15

"Very nice, Mr. Weston. I'm truly pleased that patience paid off." Mr. Wallace smiles smugly at the arrangement of dead flowers on my canvas. A cut-glass vase, half full of water, with a scattering of cut flowers on the table in front of it, a pair of shears dropped beside them, and a collection of purple and white buds against a ferny background. "Excellent perspective, and a luminous quality to the light through the glass and the water."

A photograph of the flowers in acrylic paint. Engineering-perfect lines of sight. A draftsman's still life. No impressions, no soul—no problem.

"I knew you'd get over that adolescent urge to distort things, Mr. Weston. I can see quite a future for your talent."

Check off Still Life. One certain pass.

———

"The road goes ever on, eh, Charles?" Ms. Katz cocks her head to one side and studies my landscape. A dusty road, the only hint of people in a pastoral setting. No screaming birds in the trees, no glittering windows to break the light into kaleidoscope fragments. Just leafy bushes, and a weeping willow beside a trickling stream.

"What's beyond the trees?" Ms. Katz asks suddenly.

The road disappears behind trees. There's nothing there. Emptiness, maybe. Oblivion.

"You make me want to follow the road and find out," she says thoughtfully.

Or bubbling tar pits, perhaps.

"Your composition draws the eye completely through the foreground, then inexorably down the road. Very nice."

She looks faintly troubled when I don't answer.

Earlier, in the weeks following the funeral, the teachers talked to us about death and grieving. Special counselors were available for the students. We were urged to go. I didn't. What counsel could anyone offer me? Only Adrian offered anything that made sense. The teachers looked troubled, the way Ms. Katz looks now. *Simon says... smile.* I make my mask curve upward in a smile to show her I'm pleased she likes my landscape, and she looks almost convinced. At least she turns away.

Check off Landscape. Another pass.

=====

"Interesting the way you elected to paint the model with the eyes closed, Charles. But you show us so much in the angle of the head and the line of the neck. You've certainly grown since starting here." Mr. Thornton smiles. "Where do you propose to study when you graduate?"

I grudgingly offer him a slight shrug.

"That's right—you're only a junior." He shakes his head. "What a future!"

Check off Portraiture.

≡

"I didn't think you two could beat that *Lord Jim* program, but your *Les Miserables* game is terrific."

Alona wrote it. Who knows why she shared the credit with me for just writing down ideas and passing them to her. But Ms. Cooper loved it. I decided we should give the player extra points if he succeeded in helping Javert track Jean Valjean down and arrest him before the stand at the barricades. It seemed only fair. You could argue that Javert was just doing his job in tracking down a criminal. You've always got to pay for the crime in the end.

Check off Introductory Programming. And English (extra credit for those literary computer games). And French (more extra credit for *Les Miserables*). And Government (no extra credit, just simple memorization). Check off junior year. Promote the ghost. But will Charles Weston come back to Whitman?

Get through final projects and it won't matter. . . .

≡

The studio, cool in the humid June afternoons. The only place I paint anything that matters anymore—ever, perhaps. I study the canvas, streaked with yellow ocher wash. *What does the road lead to, Ms. Katz? Perhaps this.* I concentrate on the sky, heavy with smothering clouds. I want you to feel the rain about to pelt when you look at the canvas. *Want who? "It sounds as if you've shown your work to the wrong people," Adrian said. But it's too late now. I can't show this to anyone. I should never have shown Graeme.* The ground is churned up, scruffy crabgrass matted between gnarled tree roots. I'll paint the tree later, bending its crippled branches in memory of a once and future wind. *Once wolves, now wind . . .*

Images swirl through my brain, as colors swirl in a pot of water after you plunge a handful of brushes into it, and I lose myself in them. In spite of the long afternoons, twilight fills the window before I notice the fading light. I clean my brushes slowly. I wish I could just stay in my studio, but at the same time I find myself almost looking forward to being back in the dorm room. *Someday I'll have an apartment all my own, a short hallway between studio and home, a cave to hide out in that I never have to leave.* But the old familiar wish carries only a shadow of its former comfort.

The birds scream in their leafy branches overhead as I make my way back to the dorm—they're skittish in the fading light. They'll settle down later and watch for passersby. For now, they ignore the silent ghost.

I hear the music before I open the door. "Stravinsky?" I hazard, letting myself in. *"The Firebird?"*

Adrian looks up, pleased. "You're learning."

I've learned to recognize the music he likes best, and I tell him to play it without his headphones. I say I like to listen to it. *And I do.* Small enough gestures of thanks for a friendship I don't deserve (*for not playing the game, not mentioning that night, not pressing the conversation I dreamed we had*). Sometimes I wonder if

221

he just gave me what I wanted that night (*the way Rachel tried to fix me because I wished someone could fix me, and Graeme tried to be the creator I wanted him to be*), except that the last thing I wanted was Adrian holding me. But when I tried to push him away, he wouldn't go. I'm grateful for that, as well as for the answers he offered, even if they didn't make any sense.

That doesn't matter anymore, though. I've stopped trying to make sense of anything. One evening I saw Rachel across the grass, heading toward the student center. She looked all right, and I felt a stab of relief that I hadn't hurt her—even though I knew I had. And then I wondered if I had been wrong about her that day. What if she really had accepted me—even liked me (*if she did* then, *that is*—*not that she could ever like me now, after what I've done to her*), not just acted like she cared for me because I wanted someone (*her*) to care. I used to be so sure who people were—what they were thinking. But now they seem to be more than one thing at once. Rachel only liked me because she thought I wanted her to—or Rachel liked me because she really did like me. Graeme had no self inside the mirror—or Graeme's self had always been there, he just couldn't see it. Which choice is the truth? Did the people around me change, or had I changed in what I saw? Or were they always one thing, and I saw a deception? I couldn't make sense out of any of it.

I drop my pack. "What's that?"

Adrian follows my glance to the thick envelope on my bed. "They were trying to cram it into your box downstairs, so I brought it up."

"Thanks."

He turns back to his desk, smiling, knowing I mean it.

I push the envelope to the floor beside my pack, lie back on my bed, and let the Stravinsky sweep over me. The envelope doesn't matter. It could be anything from a summer job offer as cartoonist in a local paper to an official notice that I've been expelled, and I could care less. Stravinsky writes in vivid colors—sweeping blues and oranges and vibrant reds that dance in the air. You can't listen to Stravinsky and not hear something you could paint.

I tense and blink at sudden movement, but Adrian only waves when he heads out to his studio, not interrupting the music. When it ends, I sit up regretfully, my stomach growling. I painted through supper, and I'm touched to see a sandwich and a sweating can of ginger ale waiting for me on my desk. I unwrap the sandwich and take a bite, then tear open the envelope.

A squat paperbound book drops out, along with a computer CD and a folded sheet of paper. I spread open the paper.

Charles Weston,

Along with his final manuscript, Graeme Brandt left a sheet of to-do notes that he never got a chance to act on. Among the items on the list was a reminder to himself to send you a copy of the galleys for his new book.

Because of the circumstances surrounding Graeme's death, his publisher decided to fast-track the release of the book, scheduling it for September, when young

people will be returning to school. Rather than wait
for the fall, however, I wanted to be sure you got the
galleys this spring, as soon as they were available. I do
not know whether you plan to return to Whitman next
semester.

Graeme had also set this data disc aside for you, to
accompany the galleys. I must tell you that I have tried to
open the files on the disc, but apparently they are locked.
I do not know if he gave you the key. If there is anything
on the disc that you feel I should see, I would appreciate
it if you would share the contents with me.

I trust you will find his last novel as important as I
have.

Sincerely,
Edmund Adler

I turn away from the cold letter. Mr. Adler clearly
hopes I won't come back to Whitman. Fair enough. I'm
a ghost here, anyway. I look at the compact disc, then at
the paperbound book. No slick cover, just nubbly stiff
paper with a plain title in block letters:

BREAKING THE MIRROR
a novel by
Graeme Brandt

UNCORRECTED PROOF

I open the cover—stiff, like childhood construction
paper folded over the printed pages inside. The title

page is the same. I turn the page numbly, the sandwich forgotten, and see the dedication: "To C." My stomach lurches, and I shut my eyes.

He dedicated it to me.

I slowly flip through the book, staring blankly at pages as though they're written in code, afraid to turn the spidery black letters into words, afraid to commit myself to the responsibility of reading it. *But you owe him—this is your penance.*

I pick up the metallic disc and stare at it. Locked files? I don't even know what that means.

No. Not true. No room for lying here. Ms. Cooper said something about locked files, I just didn't listen. I switch on my computer and watch the icons light up, one by one. Patterns, like puzzle pieces, across the screen. What puzzle is locked in the disc? I don't want to know.

I insert it and double-click on the icon. Only a message in a dialogue box, telling me that the disc is locked and asking me to enter the key. What key?

I stare at the blinking cursor. Why would Graeme lock the disc? *Because he didn't want anyone to see it but you.* Why didn't he just send it with the letter? *Because he wanted you to have it when you read the book.*

What is a *key*, anyway?

Alona answers her phone on the second ring.

"What's a key?"

Silence. Then, "Charles? He speaks!"

How long has it really been since I've spoken to anyone except Adrian? *Since the funeral, and after . . .*

"Yeah."

"Hi. How are you? I'm fine."

I clear my throat. "Hi. I'm lousy. What's a key?"

"As opposed to the piece of metal that gets you into your room, I suppose you mean?"

"Yeah."

"Hey—you really lousy?"

"Basically. Look—I've got a data disc that's locked. It says for me to enter a key. What's it talking about?"

"Probably the files are encrypted. Do you have an encryption program?"

"A what?"

"Describe the screen."

I tell her, and she gives a pleased sigh. "Cool. You're home free. You've got the right program. Your computer is willing to unlock the files—all you've got to do is type in the key. That's a series of characters, could be numbers or letters."

I stare blankly at the pulsing cursor. "Which? How many?"

Alona laughs. "If the person who wrote it was determined to keep everyone out, it could be up to a hundred. And they could be mixed together."

"Thanks a lot."

"Hey—it's not as bad as it sounds. Who encrypted the files? Think about a word, or a date, or a phrase that would mean something to them. People don't usually think of a key that doesn't make any sense. I mean, they might forget it. For instance, I used 'Cosette' as a key for the *Les Miserables* game while I was working on it."

"Oh."

226

"If all else fails, I've got some dis-encrypting pro-grams that might crack the code for you. But use logic first."

"I'll do that."

Alona's voice changes. "Hey, Charles—it's good to hear you. I've missed you."

I tear my eyes away from the screen and stare at the phone as if it's turned into a poisonous scorpion. "Uh—thanks."

"Yeah, well. The games were a blast—but the ques-tions you asked me about sequencing while we were planning them out, those really helped me in my own writing." She pauses. "I've been worried about you. Don't disappear into your studio forever, okay?"

I don't know what to say, and the silence stretches.

"Well—call if you can't think of the key."

"Alona—thanks. I owe you." *Why did I say that?*

"Cool. I'll collect." She sounds more cheerful as she hangs up.

What would Graeme use? The day we met? The night in his studio? I try the dates, in numbers and dig-its, backward and forward, but the computer bleeps at me: INVALID PASSWORD. I try my name, his name, Alan Travis, variations on all of them, but nothing comes up except: INVALID PASSWORD. What was he thinking?

He didn't want Mr. Adler to unlock the files. *Why?* So he wouldn't use something his mentor would recog-nize. It has to be something I'd know, only me. He meant this for me, or for no one. *A secret, like the letter.* Swiftly, I type in his suicide secret: HYPODERMIC NEEDLE,

LETHAL SOLUTION, INJECTION, all the permutations I can think of—nothing but INVALID PASSWORD. What would I know that no one else would think of?

I try DEATH. I try SUICIDE.

I try MURDER.

INVALID PASSWORD.

I think again of that morning on the roof and feel tears burn my eyes. I try MIRROR.

INVALID PASSWORD.

I see Graeme's hand smoothing out the crumpled sketch.

I type REFLECTION.

INVALID PASSWORD.

I see Graeme standing in my studio, tall and proud— a borrowed pride, reflecting what I'd hoped to see in him, but he didn't know that's what he was doing. The feeling was real for him.

I type CITYSCAPE.

The screen abruptly clears, and with a humming whir of surrender, the disc finally yields up its secrets.

16

I finish reading Graeme's journals and switch off the computer. I go to bed, the book and the relocked compact disc buried in my backpack. I don't want anyone to see them. Before I turn out the lights, I get rid of the sandwich so Adrian won't feel hurt.

I hear him come in, and watch through slitted eyelids—silver moonglow through open curtains silhouetting him—as he pauses beside me. The careful rhythm of my breathing must satisfy him because he moves away quietly, settling himself for the night. He's never asked about the day of the funeral. I don't know what he has assumed. I only know he offered friendship (*comfort*), and I accepted it. I wish I could tell him what really happened—what I read in the journals. But if he knew the truth of what I'd done to Graeme, could he still bear to know me, let alone think of himself as my friend? He said he didn't hate me, but he didn't know.... I meant to tell him everything then (*to push him away with the others*), but I couldn't.

I stare at black-and-white patterns on the inside of my lids, abstract designs that shift with the steady rumbling of his snores. I play the journal entries over and over in my mind, yearning for morning, for escape. Graeme struggled so hard in the end, but apparently he couldn't force Kyle to be someone he couldn't be himself, any more than I could paint a convincing portrait that flattered someone I knew was vicious inside. What did he end up writing in his novel, then?

When dawn brushes the sky outside my window, I rise silently and ease toward the door, carrying the pack with Graeme's book.

"Can't sleep?"

I freeze, then slowly turn around. In the pale light I see Adrian lying in bed, hands clasped behind his head. So I hadn't fooled him.

"No." My tone is a warning (*plea?*) to leave it at that.

He doesn't. "What was in the envelope?"

He sees too much with that uncanny insight of his. But we're not in the dreamlike darkness now, and I don't want to discuss it (*Graeme*) with him. I think of the uncorrected page proofs. "Proof of guilt," I say shortly.

Instead of rising to the bait, he simply asks, "Can I help?"

That's right, I think bitterly. It's all so easy for you— the wise, all-seeing roommate—the friend who understands (*forgives*) everything—the composer who lets everyone listen to his music—

"I don't know," I retort. "Can you weigh in and help prove me guilty?"

All he replies is, "Guilty of what?"

Murder, I want to scream at him, but that would betray too much (*betray Graeme's trust*). It occurs to me that I've never said anything about Graeme to Adrian—never spoken about the sketch he saw me make, any more than I ever said anything about the night of Graeme's funeral. Adrian, I suddenly realize, wasn't at the funeral.

"Destroying Graeme Brandt," I practically spit out at him.

At last his composure slips—before I know he's in motion, he's sitting upright in bed. "How could you possibly be responsible for anything to do with Graeme Brandt?"

I glare at him. "Come off it—you saw the way I sketched him. You were so pleased that it wasn't anything like as flattering as the way I drew you!" Which I know is a lie—because the sketch of Adrian was true (*is still true*), not flattering. Ashamed of the lie, I look at his desk and see the sketch still hanging above it. I stride across the room, determined finally to rip it down, but Adrian is there before me. His long fingers wrap around my left wrist as I reach for the paper.

"Don't!"

Rachel said that, too. Adrian stands before me, instead, looking defenseless in his sleep-rumpled undershirt and shorts, but he's stronger than Rachel, stronger than I ever suspected, and I can't reach past him.

"You are not responsible for anything that Graeme Brandt did," he says evenly, "but you *are* responsible for what you do here. You said that drawing was a gift. Don't take it back. Please."

For a moment I strain against him, but his grip is too strong. When I drop my arm he lets me go (*and I wish he would hold me, instead—I wish it were dark again*). When he speaks, his tone is unemotional, neither the teasing lilt nor the comforting voice of the night. "You drew him as a mirror. How could that destroy him?"

I can't meet his eyes. "Graeme believed me. I told him he was nothing but a lifeless mirror—I told him he was dead, and he believed me."

Adrian doesn't say anything for a moment. Then he asks, again, "What proof was in that envelope?"

I stare down at the mottled tan dorm carpet. "Something Graeme left for me," I mutter, not wanting to explain the locked disc. "And his last book."

"Graeme arranged to tell you that you had destroyed him *before* his heart attack?" Adrian asks, his tone disbelieving. "I mean—it's monstrous that he should plan to reach out from beyond the grave in order to blame you for—for whatever he did." He shakes his head. "And you just *accept* his saying you're guilty?"

I look up, furious at his outraged incredulity. I want him to know the truth—I want him to know what I did—I want to push him away as absolutely as I've pushed everyone else away (*but—everyone else chose to turn on me, didn't they? I didn't choose to push them away—I wanted to belong with them. Or did I really want to be alone all along?*) Before I stop to think, I say, my voice harsh, "It wasn't a heart attack. He made it look like one, but he killed himself, all right? He saw my paintings, and he killed himself!"

Adrian's eyes widen and he takes a step back from

me. *Good—now you hate me, too—now you'll leave me alone, like all the rest.*

As I jerk open the door I think I hear him call my name, but I must be imagining it. I'm out of the dorm and running. Not my studio. I go to the roof and sit propped against the parapet siding, remembering Graeme sitting cross-legged on the gravel beside me. A different morning. (*But I had still run away from everyone—from Adrian.*) I open the book and look again at Graeme's dedication to me. I take a deep breath and read.

Hours later, I close the book. If I'd never read his first novel, I think this one would have moved me even more, but it would never have brought me to Whitman, because I would have known the author could never answer my question. But where do I go from here?

It's too late to throw the envelope into the trash, unopened and unread. Too late to decide I can't unlock the disc and read Graeme's secret files. Too late to pretend I never cared about Graeme's legacy, his brilliant books, and his ruined hope. I've reawakened (*pushed Adrian away, like everyone I dare to let get close to me*). I can't turn back the clock to become yesterday's ghost, alive only in his world of paint. I want to run downstairs to my studio and lock the door and forget Graeme's book as I managed to forget everything else (*the dead look in his eyes on the roof, the pain in Rachel's voice as her kaleidoscope shattered*), but I never really forgot. I only went into hiding, painting stillborn life studies for fools like Mr. Wallace, blindfolding my soul the way I silenced my speech.

Now, painfully, my mind is thinking again, prodding the scars, telling me flatly that I can't go on pretending there's no world (*no Rachel, no Alona, no consequences to pay for the pain I've caused*) outside of my studio and the unspoken lies that made Adrian befriend me (*not anymore—not now that I've put the truth into words that even he had to hear*). Painfully, I touch the textured paper cover on the book I just finished reading. People like Graeme live outside my studio, in that world. And he tried so hard....

In Graeme's book, Kyle wanted to break the mirror, to stop being only what people like his brother and classmates and teachers wanted him to be, but he couldn't. He couldn't work out who to be, so he kept trying to create a role for himself, but none of them fit. He didn't know where to find a role that worked, except from someone else.

Kyle Travis was Graeme from this spring on the page, just as Alan Travis had been the Graeme of three years ago.

But Kyle wasn't the only character trying to change his pattern in this book. Morgan was the school yearbook photographer, and he didn't have a life beyond his photos. He was a shadow in the school, bumped by the other kids in the hallways, but mostly ignored—except by Kyle. Kyle was fascinated by him. As things got worse, as Kyle felt an emptiness growing inside him and none of the roles he tried was enough to fill it, he turned on Morgan. He dragged Morgan into his circle of friends on the pretext of wanting him to join their gang (and you could see just how Morgan would be suckered into it, wanting to fit in somewhere) and humiliated him—ripped him so badly that Morgan dropped out of school. Maybe he transferred somewhere—he dropped out of the book, anyway.

I knew Morgan was me, whether Graeme meant him to be or not. But he got the ending wrong. I wasn't the one who got destroyed—he was.

Or did we destroy each other?

I hug my knees, staring at the blurring parapet across the roof. I may have killed Graeme, but I killed something in myself as well. I'm less than I was when I came here. At least then I had hoped to find some answers. Now I've given up hope. I know (*in spite of Adrian saying he doesn't hate me, in spite of Alona telling me not to disappear in my studio forever*) I'm beyond redemption. I can't ever pay for what I did to Graeme, or to Rachel. I don't dare show my paintings to anyone, ever again.

Why did Graeme leave me his journals and his book? To finish the destruction, or to set me free?

To punish you for killing him...

I stand up abruptly, my stiff legs crying out in protest, and limp away from the book and the disc toward the far parapet. The familiar guilt is too easy, easier than facing what we really did to each other. And suddenly, standing beside the parapet, almost the shadow in my painting come to life, I feel a surge of anger wash over me—not anger at myself, for once—anger at Graeme Brandt.

You *choose* to play Simon Says, and you can choose to *stop*! Graeme chose to play and, worse, he chose to

235

make me his Simon (*blame me*). I wanted him to tell me how to do what I dreamed of doing (*God—did I want to give in to the game all along?*), but I never wanted to tell him what to do with his life! He had no right to make me responsible for his death—*it's monstrous that he should blame you*—he had no right to give up! Those two books—that insight that brought me here—the potential they represent—what else could he have written, if he had given himself the chance to grow up? What else could he have written if he had been brave enough to try living, instead of dying?

I grind my palms into the concrete top of the parapet, stopping short of drawing my own blood this time. *Blood pays for blood.* But it's not blood I owe him—or that he owed me. Graeme owed me more than a dedication and his journals. He owed me (*he owed himself*) an honest try at starting over—at finding out who he really was inside and learning how to be true to that self. So what if it wasn't easy? So what if it didn't happen in the space of a few months, in the writing of one book? You try every day, pushing yourself and digging deeper. You don't just take the easy way out and give up, even if you have to cripple one part of yourself to keep growing. Unless there's nowhere to grow.

I'm back to the question I asked myself when I found out he was writing: Do we choose who we are, or are we born that way? If Graeme was born a mirror, *could* he choose to change? Or did he choose to be a mirror, and could he have chosen to grow in a new direction? Adrian said (*he said it's monstrous—he said he didn't hate you—but does he still feel that way?*) you choose to change as you see things about yourself you like or don't like. Couldn't Graeme have chosen differently—have seen himself differently?

I go back and shove *Breaking the Mirror* into my pack with the disc. Then I pull out my old sketch pad from last fall. I left it in my pack all this time, until I knew how to finish the sketch I'd begun. *Something else I had made myself forget after his death...* The breeze flutters the pages as I flip through them to the drawing of Graeme—of his book, rising inspired from my painting. *Could you have changed, or were you always a mirror?* But the sketch is as lifeless as ever, and I suddenly rip it from the pad, shredding it and letting the kaleidoscope fragments scatter in the wind. The answers I'm looking for can't be found on this rooftop.

I climb down the stone stairs, head out of the building, out into the mid-morning rush of kids hurrying between classes. What am I missing? It doesn't matter. I've completed all my final projects and gotten the passes taken care of. No one will miss the ghost cutting class for once.

I take off across the campus, outside it, two blocks to the church, and then around back to the quiet churchyard where Graeme's grave is grown over with thick grass and decorated with fresh flowers propped against an austere tombstone bearing only his name, the years of his life, and the chiseled words: BELOVED SON AND AUTHOR. A Whitman legend already, just as he wanted. Or was he ever the one who really wanted that?

I reach into my pack, take out the letter Graeme wrote me before he killed himself, and read it again.

Then I stare at the gently mounded earth, asking the spirit that lingers there if it really had always been only a mirror. He had written, *It must be wanting something, knowing what you want. But everything I wanted was what someone else told me to want.* His version of Simon Says... (*But Adrian says there aren't any games... or if it is all a game, then artists are the real Simons—offering good choices, not destroying the other players.*) And Graeme *did* want things. In his journal he wrote about how much he wanted to play baseball, until his mother told him he shouldn't. That was wanting something. Or did he only like baseball because his friend, Mike somebody, wanted him to like it?

Except— There *was* something he wanted, wasn't there? I don't need a computer screen to remember his journals—he wrote that he wanted readers to look at things from a new perspective. He wanted to show them things they hadn't known before. And he did that in his two books. I swallow, finally seeing the true magnitude of his waste. Graeme didn't just want to reflect other people's ideas in his writing. What mattered to him was showing new ideas—new perspectives. And he accomplished that. Only he never realized it.

He told me on the rooftop that he showed his readers what they were doing and who they were in his books, so they'd stop and think about themselves. I think of the way I show what to reach for in my paintings, and remember Steve telling me that they made him uncomfortable because they demanded too much. Maybe my paintings don't speak to everyone—maybe

Graeme's books speak to people who would turn away from my paintings. His books don't tell them what to strive for, but if it makes them think about who they are and change themselves because they aren't who they wanted to be, isn't that the same effect? And he would have gone on finding new ways to make readers think, if he hadn't killed himself.

"You shouldn't have accepted that there were only two possibilities open to you," I say out loud, as if his spirit could still hear me, "either my judgment, or the empty reflection you let the world make you into. You should have fought harder to find a way to live up to your writing, the way I try to live up to my paintings. I came here wanting to change, even if I didn't know how."

And suddenly I realize that Graeme may have decided he couldn't change (*decided wrongly, because he did have so much more to give—it's a mistake he can't ever take back*), but his journals and his books were showing me a different idea—they were telling me that *I* could change. He didn't want me to stay hidden in my studio. He thought he couldn't be the person (*creator*) he wanted to be in the end (*the person I wanted him to be—yes, but he wanted it, too*), and he chose to kill himself because he couldn't go on living with the emptiness (*and he wasn't empty—if he'd only held on, he could have found the self inside, the self that reached out to his readers and showed them ideas they hadn't thought about before—the self he always wanted to be, and was*). But even if he couldn't see it in himself, he could see that I wasn't empty. I'm afraid, but I'm not empty. He was telling me I could let the Kyles of the world lock me away forever, or I could set myself free.

When have you felt most alive, Charles?

When Graeme Brandt stood in my studio and looked at my paintings.

You're right, Graeme. I can't hide forever.

I sit down beside his grave, confessing the real secret of my heart that I'd kept hidden. The sketch I made of you wasn't a lie, but it was only a moment's truth—sketches are transitory, because who you are at any moment is only one step on the road of who you become. I've made myself stay that masked Harlequin for far too long. You didn't have to stay a mirror forever. When you decided you didn't like that image, it wasn't too late to change. But my true guilt is deeper. Instead of showing you that momentary sketch first, I should have let you see my paintings. Paintings are eternal because they're a promise of what might be, and that potential is always somewhere ahead of you, forever possible and forever worth striving for.

Suppose you'd seen my paintings when your mother and your teachers were trying to mold you into their idea of a writer, and your father was trying to mold you into his idea of the perfect son—when they were all teaching you to play Simon Says? Could you have shown them your real self then, instead of reflecting back the image they wanted? And even though you didn't see my paintings until too late, even though you didn't believe you had a real self, you *did* have a self buried deep inside the heart of the kaleidoscope—a self that was straining to get out, and you put that self—your ideas—into your books. You've left behind a legacy that will make a difference to everyone who reads them, who understands them. You left me a legacy, too—the demand that I admit the truth.

If I died today, who would be better for my having lived? No one. I think of my paintings, of my hope in asking Steve to look at them, of my pride in showing them to Cindy, of my pleasure and shame at my father's hanging that football painting in his office, of my longing for my parents to really look at my paintings and understand them. I always meant for my work to be seen.

I think of my father hopefully extolling the possibilities of computer programming, and my mother looking away from my paintings, and I ache with wishing I'd kept on showing them my real work until they accepted it—and accepted me. Why didn't I? Why weren't they out in the open for Graeme to see?

Mother says . . . paint happy pictures, Charlie, pictures that won't make people nervous. Keep the other pictures to yourself. Comforting words when I was little and the other kids made fun of me, then called me names, then finally looked at me strangely and pushed me away. Comforting words for a mother who doesn't want her friends to think there's something wrong with her because she has an artistic son. But I'm no longer a child to do what Mother says. *You're not a little boy anymore, Charlie—painting pictures is fine for a hobby—* I'm *not* a little boy anymore, and I've got to find a way to take responsibility for myself—for my art. It's not just a hobby. It's never been a hobby. It's my life.

And they were never comforting words, were they? *Simon says . . . keep your art separate, keep it safe from the people who laugh at you or sneer at you, who resent your drawings—* It wasn't me keeping my art safe—ever—any more than it was Graeme becoming his own person by taking his own life. He made me into his Simon so that I could take the blame for his wasted future. And I let my mother be my Simon— Or did I *make* her be my Simon, telling me what to do? Instead of her being entirely responsible for being disappointed in the son she's got, did I somehow make her feel that she had to tell me how to behave? Did Graeme *make* his mother into the domineering voice who told him to be a writer, and did I make mine into a barricade against the hurt?

The simple tombstone shudders and blurs through a gray wash of tears until there are two tombstones—one for Graeme's body, one for the lost hopes we both share. I shake my head. Does *everyone* play Simon Says? Was Rachel trying to fix me because I expected her to? Do we all react to each other's expectations, even when we think we're not?

And then it comes to me, like a silver-plucked violin note hanging in the air. Not everyone.

I blink away the tears, put the folded letter carefully away in my pack, and climb stiffly to my feet, my anger at Graeme for casting me as his Simon slowly bleeding away like the colors draining from a paintbrush dipped in turpentine. It was his fault for looking for Simons everywhere, for believing there had to be someone else telling him who he was. It was his fault for believing me, and wasting everything he could have become—that insight, that shining potential. But he was right—I was doing it, too. I listened way too long even when I thought I was screaming defiance in paint. I listened to the voice condemning me to isolation, and I did what I was told. There's only one person I know who doesn't listen to any Simon.

Perhaps Graeme wasn't the one I came here to meet after all. Perhaps it isn't too late to ask the question I came to Whitman to get answered.

17

I feel my feet moving, leaving Graeme's escape behind, thudding across the pavement, back onto campus, running through the soft grass, past staring strangers, to corridors of practice rooms beneath the concert hall. I stumble to a halt under soundproofed ceilings, scanning the room numbers, muffled bass beats throbbing around me. *Well, if you get stranded in the rain before reaching your safe haven, you can always dry off in 207 downstairs—I leave it unlocked.* The closest door says 221, and I hurry down the crowded hallway before I lose my nerve.

When I turn the handle of 207 and pull the door open, music swirls into the hall, exuberant red-gold chords dancing from the piano. Heads turn in the hallway, but the faces aren't glaring at me for letting the noise out. Instead, they light up at the joy in the rippled notes. I step into a room cluttered with stacks of sheet music and bulging notebooks and stray CDs and even a dusty sweatshirt wadded up against the baffled cork walls, and ease the door shut behind me. The hall and the faces disappear and even the clutter fades until there's nothing but me and the piano and the figure bent over the keyboard, releasing that radiant music. Adrian.

I think of his courage in letting his quartet be performed, in risking Tyler's reviews, in learning from the teachers here instead of hiding from them. I remember him coming back after Christmas vacation, hurt again by his parents' disapproval, sharp-tongued for a few weeks but refusing to lose himself or pretend to be something he's not. There are some things about yourself you can't choose to change, but you can change how you choose to live that self—stillborn, or all the way.

The music reaches its climax and dances to its finish, then his hands come to rest on the keys. For a moment his hazel eyes are unfocused. A smile plays softly across his lips like his music's lingering echo, and I stare, unable to speak. It's my sketch come to life—the face lit with love for the music that the mind and the heart have created. I'm stunned at my blindness in not seeing that he was the person I was looking for all this time—and shocked at how wrong I had been about that night at the party after the one-acts. Adrian didn't misunderstand either sketch, not for a moment. He didn't suspect that my sketch of him betrayed feelings that were different from my feelings for Graeme. He recognized himself in the way I sketched him. So he knew that if I could see inside of him, I could see inside of Graeme as well and find the emptiness there. He'd probably seen it long before. Adrian had never crowded around Graeme with the other admirers.

He sees me and blinks, his expression suddenly clouding. Oh God—did I succeed in pushing him away this morning? Is it too late after all?

"Charles?" His voice is wary, but not angry, as he half rises from the piano bench. "Are you all right?"

Thank you for not hating me. Now—please be the one I'm searching for. "How can I do it?" I ask unsteadily, now that I'm finally poised on the parapet's brink for real. "Can you tell me how?"

He sinks back down, one arm resting protectively across his keyboard, frowning slightly. "Tell you how to do what?"

I ask the question at last. "How can I show my paintings?"

Adrian doesn't turn away from me in disgust. He doesn't repeat the answers he gave me in the dark—they were only the beginning. He studies me in silence for a long heartbeat. Then he says, "Well, if it's anything like music, you're so excited about it that you play it for people who let you down by hating it. Or by hating you for writing it."

I've done that. I look down at my knuckles and see how white they are. Somewhere, in a different studio, a high string note soars hauntingly.

"But you already know that part, don't you?" he asks. "It's not the end, though. The music won't go out of your head, so you keep playing it—you play it for someone else who's blown away, and you know inside that they're making too much of it, but at the same time you can't help hoping they're not."

I think of Graeme standing transfixed in my studio.

He exaggerated my paintings in his journal—I know they're not masterpieces; they're not that deep, not yet, anyway. But I have it in me to become that good, that deep, in time, if I open up and let myself learn more. I feel a smile starting to build inside of me.

"And then, because it sounds so right to you," Adrian goes on, "you keep playing it, and writing new stuff, and playing that. And after a while, you stop listening to the Tylers, and to the people who make too much of it, and to anything except the song inside of you and the voices of people who can help you make it truer. And pretty soon, you're not asking *how* can I, any longer, but *who else* can I play it for."

I nod. That's what I want—to keep painting, and to listen to the people who can show me how to become better. "Thank you." And then, "I'm sorry—about your sketch this morning. I lied." In a rush, "It wasn't flattery—it was true—it *is* a true drawing."

He smiles suddenly, and I realize he's matching the smile on my face.

In the end, can forgiveness be that easy? Except… "But how can you just stop listening to the people who hate you for what you can do, for who you are—who want you to be someone else? How can you ever get close to anyone, if they all want you to be—well, who they imagined? Who Simon says you should be? Like—your parents who don't want you to write music—or be gay…" My voice trails off.

He looks away for a moment, flushing. Then he shrugs one shoulder. "Well, I just try to keep telling myself that not everyone's perfect. I'm certainly not. Other people aren't, either, especially if they choose to play Simon Says. But whether they play games or not, they can love you and still not be able to understand you. All you can do is accept that and love them back and not expect too much. I mean"—he chuckles faintly—"you can't give up, and you can't give in, can you? I just tell myself that one day I'll find someone who loves my music, and me, for myself."

Could it really be that simple? Just not giving up and not giving in? In the end, does it come down to me accepting myself?

I think it does.

I smile at him. "Want to see something?"

He cocks his head to one side. "What?"

"Unless you're in the middle of something," I say, suddenly remembering how I burst into his practice room.

He laughs, a sound as happy as his music. "That was only my composition project, and it's finished—graded and everything. I was just playing it because I like it."

My smile turns into a grin. "Come on."

Adrian hesitates a moment, then nods. We walk back down his hallway, side by side, and he smiles or jokes with students as we go by—not just strange faces to him, but people he's taken the trouble (*risk*) to know. We cross the quad to my studio building, climb the stone stairs, reach my locked door. I undo the hasp lock, heft it for a moment, then slide the key into its slot and lean around the corner to toss the pair of them down the stairs. Let someone else lock themselves away from life.

Adrian pauses in the hallway. "Charles—you don't have to—"

But I do. Graeme asked me, *What do you want, Charles? It must be wanting something, knowing what you want.* And Adrian just told me, *Pretty soon, you're not asking* how can I any longer, *but* who else *can I play it for.* To me that translates into: Who else can I show? This is what I want—what I've always wanted, even though I hid from it for so long. To show my paintings. To whom? To my friends, to start with. To Adrian. *What did you really want, Graeme? I think you wanted to make a difference to people when you wanted to show them new ideas, new perspectives—maybe you became a writer because your mother told you to, but what you chose to do with your writing was up to you. And you did make a difference—to me.*

I push open the door. "Come in."

And then I stand there watching him. I've only felt this way—this mixture of hope and fear and joy at being me—once before, for real, when Graeme stood where Adrian is now. But Adrian's expression is different. He doesn't look astounded; he looks like he's come home, like he belongs here. I realize I'm going to paint him. I want to capture the rusty halo of his hair.

"And this is only the beginning," I tell him.

He looks up, smiling, from the painting of the figure striding beneath the cluster of restless birds. "What next?"

"I'm going to show them, and sell them—well, if anyone will buy them." Then— "Except one. The cityscape."

I remember Graeme's face, gazing at it. His key. "That one's bought and paid for."

Adrian's smile dims, and he looks away. Perhaps my outburst this morning still hurts him. Perhaps you have to earn forgiveness over time. I'm willing to do that.

He turns to the draped easel and lifts the cloth, revealing the unfinished painting of the shadow on the parapet. Cocking his head to one side, he studies the abyss that waits below. Somehow I couldn't force the shadow to fall. "Graeme was wrong to try to make you responsible for his decision, whatever actually happened," he says quietly. "We all make choices along the way toward figuring out who we really are, but we have only ourselves to blame if the choice is a mistake. Usually we can try to make up for it." *I will*, I promise myself, and Graeme's spirit.

Adrian nods toward the painting. "If the shadow crashes, he gives up on the future. Graeme chose to give up, and it was a horrible mistake that he can't undo." Then he turns to me. "But I don't think this one's giving up. I think he's going to soar through the clouds and come out the other side." He pauses. "And whatever Graeme may have written to you—he didn't make his choice because he saw these." He sweeps his arm around the studio. "Your paintings are a promise of *life*, not death."

My voice sounds choked as I tell him, "The city-scape—it was a long time ago." I clear my throat, realizing the truth in my words. "He was blown away." But Adrian isn't—he's the one whose vision has always been true, even truer than my own. I'm grateful to him for echoing my conclusions about Graeme—and even more grateful for his faith in my future. "When you see one that speaks to you, it's yours." I grin at his expression of delighted surprise, and start out of the studio. "Well, you were the one who showed me what Simon Says really was, the only one who knew."

"But I said you didn't need to play." He looks puzzled when I glance back.

"You told me an artist would be Simon, doing the saying," I remind him. "I think..." I pause, working it out in my mind. "I think some people know who they are and what they want out of life, but others aren't sure. They're going to look for somebody to tell them what to do, or tell them who they are. And not all of them are artists," I point out ruefully. "I can testify to that." But I didn't have to let the kids and teachers chase me away. I didn't have to strike out with my sketches. That was just another way of crippling myself.

I go on, "I think we need a lot of Simons, offering lots of different options. If somebody who isn't sure of himself hears only one Simon saying what to do, then he'll do it. But if he hears a lot of them, then he's forced to choose the option that feels right, and he'll start to find himself."

Now Adrian grins. "Come on, Charles. With these paintings shouting so triumphantly, do you really think anyone's going to listen to any other artist Simons?"

"They'll listen to them. But maybe they won't decide to do what they say."

I feel so incredibly full of life that I'm bouncing off the walls. How did I ever manage to stay inside this room for so long?

"I've got to get out of here—there's so much to do." I gesture at the images surrounding him. "You take your time."

Smiling, he flutters the fingers of his right hand in a cheerful wave and turns back to the paintings. I no longer wonder why he acts like that. Adrian knows who he is, and he isn't about to reflect anyone else's expectations. Good for him. "I'll see you later," I promise.

As I hurry down the tiled hallway, through the press of strangers I suddenly wish I'd taken the trouble to get to know, I imagine Adrian's pleasure when I tell him that I want to paint him. And I wonder which painting he'll pick for his own.

I head for the student center, knowing the offices will be open. I can feel a grin stretching crazily across my face. *I'm going to show my paintings!* Then I catch sight of the bank of phones in the front hall. I grab the receiver and make a collect call. I can't stop smiling.

Not the machine this time, or my mother's office— where I'll hear her guarded, cautious voice shying away from my paintings because I haven't made her look at them, only feeling safe talking about my grades, about her college hopes for me, about the future she wants for a son who conforms to her image. Instead, I call my father's office—where I'll find a parent who's at least trying to reconcile my art with the dreams he's had for his son. *You can't give up, and you can't give in, can you?* His secretary accepts the charges.

"Charles—what's wrong?" My father's voice is tight and sharp. I can picture him standing at his desk, his face drawn with worry, staring at the painted football receiver straining for the ball in defiance of the defenders who want to crush him.

"Nothing. Not a single thing. Not now." Surely he can hear the grin in my voice. "Dad—I want you and Mom to come to Whitman when the semester's over." *They'd wanted to take me here last fall, but I wouldn't let them. Will they come now?* "I want you to meet my friends." *I want you to meet Adrian, and Alona. And Rachel?* "I want you to meet my teachers." *I'll give Ms. Katz the wind-crippled tree for a final project. Then she'll know where the road leads. Even if Mr. Wallace never gets it, I think she might. And maybe I can learn something from her after that—next semester.* "And Dad—" I pause. "I want you to see my studio. My paintings," I add, in case he didn't understand.

"Charles—"

I hear relief in his voice, and guarded pleasure. Maybe he'll be proud of me for real, even if he can't fully understand. Maybe they both will. I'll just have to give them the chance.

Finally, I climb the stairs, avoiding the groaning elevator. I walk past the windows and push open the door to the *Ventures* office. The same girl stares at me, probably wearing the same stretched-out T-shirt. "Yeah?"

"Hi, Buffy," I tell her, that crazy grin exploding all over the place. "Where's Rachel?"

She tries to tell me I have to wait, that Rachel is busy.

"Hey—I've waited too long, Buffy. Trust me—I'm way late to see her."

The puzzles are back in their places. Kaleidoscopes pick up flickers of light from the narrow window. Rachel's face is wary now—the long swept-away fragments of the shattered kaleidoscope still lie between us. But my chest tightens again at the sight of her, and I wonder if it's not too late, after all. I'm willing to take the time to earn her forgiveness.

"I'm sorry," I tell her, simply. "I—I didn't mean to hurt you. I was angry at myself, and I took it out on you." Words can't make up for my actions, but she deserves them. Whether she tried to fix me because she thought that's what I wanted her to do, or whether the impulse really came from within, the way Adrian's comfort did, doesn't matter in the end. What she did was her choice. What I did was mine, and I have to accept responsibility for it.

Perhaps she realizes intuitively what I'm thinking. Her eyes focus on me in a different way, suddenly—dissecting me. But that doesn't frighten me now.

"You once said you wanted to print one of my paintings. I should have listened to you." *It would still have been too late for Graeme... He chose to let it be too late, after all.* "Would you like to print one now?"

Her eyes light up. If she still wants the painting for *Ventures* then she still wants to look inside me, take me apart, analyze my potential, and edit me into shape. Fair enough. Maybe I can withstand her scrutiny as long as she helps my paintings be seen—there'll be time enough after that to work out my relationships with other people, beyond painting. I think of Graeme standing in my studio, of Adrian's smile. How will Rachel react? And I wonder what Alona will say when she sees my work. *Cool—you're home free.*

Rachel is talking about layouts and the deadline for the graduation issue. She wants a photographer in my studio now, yesterday, at least this afternoon.

"Whenever's fine," I tell her.

I can't undo the hurt—I was part of what killed Graeme and I may have broken something in Rachel, too. But I'm not facing a dead end any longer. I don't have to keep looking back, to resurrect the crippled sketch artist in his Harlequin mask. I've redrawn myself this morning. I believe I really can soar through the clouds and come out the other side.

I stand for a few minutes outside the student center, alone but not isolated. I do belong at Whitman—but more than that. I belong in my parents' home, and in this world—in all the worlds around me. And they belong to me. They're mine to transform through paint, to share with the people I care about.

I promise I will find the courage to show my paintings, and I will use them to inspire people to change this world of expectations that made Graeme believe he had no choice but to kill himself. I promise them all—Graeme's spirit, Adrian, Rachel, Alona, my parents, everyone I have yet to meet.

But most of all, I promise myself.

ACKNOWLEDGMENTS

This book has been many years in the writing—and rewriting—and I would like to thank the numerous people who helped bring it to life. I wrote the first version during my senior year in college, and I would like to thank my roommate, Karla Painter (who always wanted to see more of Adrian), and my friend Susan Taylor for participating in late-night brainstorming sessions and offering such discerning insights at the birth of these characters. I appreciate my parents, Richard and Janice Bonilla, for the inspiration they gave me. I am grateful to my Rice professors, particularly J. Dennis Huston, Terrence Doody, Sandy Havens, and Frank E. Vandiver, who believed in me and pushed me to grow as a writer.

I would like to thank early readers Tom Reveley, William Goyen, and George Williams for their comments and encouragement. As I grew as a writer and *Simon Says* grew as a book, I received invaluable critical help from the members of my critique group, Pamela F. Service, Marilyn D. Anderson, Elsa Marston, Pat McAlister,

Keiko Kasza, and Marcia Kruchten. I would also like to thank later readers Charles A. Finn III, James M. Janik, and Jean Gralley for their thoughtful feedback.

When I was striving to launch my writing career, I received generous encouragement and heartfelt advice from Stephen Sondheim, who urged me to believe in my vision for this book, but warned that I would have a hard time finding a publisher who was willing to gamble on a complex, demanding novel that kept the reader thinking as the work unfolded. Then he added that it was better for me to realize this so young than to break my heart at forty-five over the discovery—a prophetic comment, until Harcourt decided it was willing to take the gamble. I would especially like to thank my editor, Karen Grove, and managing editor, Lynn Harris, who have been committed to *Simon Says* from their first reading. I cannot imagine an editor who could have been more dedicated, asked better questions, or offered wiser guidance in shaping this book than Karen.

Finally, I would like to thank my husband, Arthur B. Alphin, who listened patiently to the story of this book on our first date—and went on to support me unfailingly as I pursued my dream of showing my own work to readers. Although this is my only published book written before I met him, his love and faith in me have become an integral part of its final version.